George Sand

The enchanted Lake

A Tale

George Sand

The enchanted Lake
A Tale

ISBN/EAN: 9783337136796

Printed in Europe, USA, Canada, Australia, Japan

Cover: Foto ©Andreas Hilbeck / pixelio.de

More available books at **www.hansebooks.com**

THE

ENCHANTED LAKE,

A TALE

BY GEORGE SAND

MEMOIR.

HERE is a difficult and mysterious subject. There has been so much philosophy used in talking of the author of *Lelia*, that I may no doubt be allowed to make my *debut* with a light, and I hope not a wearisome narration, whose only merit is its authenticity.

A few days ago, I was labouring under a painful sleep; I was sinking under the weight of a biographical nightmare; from the like of which may heaven protect my reader! for it is the most atrocious of all nightmares! when I was roused suddenly to receive a letter which I opened mechanically; it ran thus:

"Madame Dudevant (that is the legal name of George Sand) wishes you to call on her for a *small order* that she has to give you." Here followed the direction and the hour when to call.

I again read the note; I rubbed my eyes; it seemed to me very evident that I was awake; and yet the contents of the note completely upset me. I know well, in good sooth, some few old out of date mortals who would willingly have me, and *order* a biography; it is done often; but I never take *orders* of that sort: George Sand could never give me one.

I lost myself in conjecturing, when the thought came across me (I must have been stupid or asleep not to have looked before,) to glance at the superscription; it was addressed to M. M——, *Poëlier fumiste.** The mystery was thus explained. Deceived by a certain resemblance in the name, George Sand's Mercury, who was no doubt a subtle son of Savoy, and my porter, who was a no less stupid one of the mountains of Auvergne, had made it all right at once; they had perhaps read somewhere the charming lines of Voltaire about *the smoke and the glory;* and they had judiciously concluded, that between a *fumiste* and a biographer of celebrated contemporaries, there is not, to use a phrase of M. Viennet, *the diameter of the earth*; and thanks to the similarity of appellations, I found myself in pos-

* *Poëlier fumiste* is a trade unknown in this country; they are men that arrange the exit of the smoke from the stoves, so much in use on the continent.

tession of an autograph destined for a kind of colleague.

"Happy *fumiste!*" said I, at first thinking of sending him the note; "you will see genius in dishabille; genius makes no show before a workman of your species; it always does more or less before a biographer! After all, why should I not be a *fumiste?* Can I not be a *fumiste* and biographer by turns? I have known lawyers without number who have risen to be statesmen; I have some notion of chemistry; I have too an *encyclopædia of the arts and sciences*; I will study the article *fumée*, and then I shall know how much to believe, when the world begins its fantastic narrations concerning the author of *Lelia*. They have talked about her fierce and fascinating look; of her loud but solemn voice; they have told me that she lived, like a hermit, on a high spot that can only be reached by a ladder; and I have also read in a *St. Petersburgh Gazette* that she is five feet six inches in height, that her hair forms a shawl to cover her shoulders, that she wears a pointed hat cocked on one ear, mustachios, and boots and spurs withal.

"But as I am by nature rather sceptical, all that seems to me rather apocryphal; and I see the clearer, that nothing is known concerning her, except that she is a great writer, and that the stove flue of her habitation is out of order. What an excellent opportunity to ascertain the rest!"

Once the idea in my head, there it remained; the call was fixed for the same day; the style of the letter indicated that the person addressed was not known to the writer. I got up, dressed myself in haste; I stood before the glass, and I perceived with pleasure that I had just hit the necessary elegance requisite for a sweep; I read the article on *fumée*, I put in my pocket an elegant two-foot rule, and I set out determined to brave all difficulties rather than let the opportunity escape which placed in my hands the necessary details for writing the biography of a person,—one especially that would be so eagerly sought after as that of George Sand.

I soon arrived at the end of the Chaussée d'Antin, in a silent and solitary street that I will not name, because I am neither a Court Guide nor a Blue Book. I entered a house of fine appearance. They conducted me through a garden: at the end of the garden, to the right, they showed me a little isolated pavilion. I knocked at the door of this pavilion; they opened it, and then made me ascend a flight of stairs, and I thus found myself in a little anti-chamber.

I was then asked my name. I hesitated an instant; but calling to my aid my biographical fanaticism, I borrowed the name of the honest *fumiste*, who little dreamt that I was at that moment personating him. They begged of me to wait. In truth it was what I wanted; for I had hardly had time to learn my part, and I wished sadly to rehearse it before the first representation.

Although they kept me waiting a length of time, I felt my first ardour ooze away unaccountably. The part I was playing had only been viewed by me on the advantageous side: all the disadvantages now presented themselves before me. I saw a child, with light curly hair, continually pass and repass, whose inquisitive glance made me very uneasy; 't was Mademoiselle Solange, the pretty daughter of the illustrious writer; and to make me still more uncomfortable, I fancied I heard on the other side of the door the voice of an artist who knew me well; and I repeated to myself: "if I am discovered I shall make but a very sorry figure." And certainly the prospect of having a chimney to sweep, taking into consideration my inexperience, was rather alarming. On the other side, having gone so far it would have been a pity to back out.

In this perplexity, I resolved suddenly to address myself to the duenna who had let me in. I thought it was no doubt that worthy *Ursule*, mentioned in *Lettres d'un Voyageur*, that mistook Switzerland for

Cape Martinico, and that thought gave me a little
assurance; and I then related the *quid-pro-quo* that
induced me to make the visit, and I added in a mild
tone, that I was merely an amateur of strange ad-
ventures, and under that title would be glad to have
an interview with her mistress; and if she were
willing to aid me, I would only be too happy to
offer her a complete set of my works. This offer
seemed to flatter her sensibly, for she smiled agree-
ably on me, and glided mysteriously into the sanc-
tuary, making me a sign which seemed to say "wait."
And I, trembling, awaited the coming of the tall,
the terrible *Lelia*, recommending my soul to all the
saints in Paradise. I heard soon after some chairs
disturbed, and an energetical address on the stu-
pidity of her waiting women. It came nearer; and
presently the door opened, and I shut my eyes,
quite overcome with fear.

When I re-opened them, I saw before me a woman
under the middle height, and rather stout. She
wore a dressing gown, something like the one I have
in use myself; beautiful hair, still perfectly black,
(notwithstanding what the evil tongues say) parted
on a large forehead as smooth as a mirror, and falling on her cheeks after the manner of Raphael; a
silk handkerchief was negligently tied round her
neck : her look, which some artists make terrible,

had a remarkable expression of melancholy softness; the sound of her voice was agreeable and subdued; her mouth too was singularly pleasing; and there was in all her demeanour a striking picture of simplicity, calmness, and grandeur. From the fulness of the temples, and the fine development of the forehead, Spurzheim would have predicted genius: from the pure features of her face, Lavater would have said: "an unhappy past, the present still bitter; but with all, extreme enthusiasm." Lavater might have read much more, but he would not have traced on that placid, yet melancholy face, either bitterness, hate, or chicanery. The *Lelia* of my imagination vanished before the stern reality; and it was only a good, gentle, melancholy, intelligent, fine figure, that I had before mine eyes.

In continuing my examination, I remarked with pleasure that the great authoress had not entirely renounced the frivolities of this world, for under the cuffs of her morning dress, between her wrist and a fine delicate hand, I saw two bracelets of exquisite workmanship. It appeared feminine; and had a good effect. It reassured me a good deal; particularly with respect to the politico-philosophical works which the last writings of George Sand savour completely of. One of the hands I examined hid a cigarette, and badly hid it too; for the tell-tale wreaths of smoke kept ascending behind the arm of the celebrated authoress.

I hope it is well understood that during this examination my tongue kept continually wagging. Quite re-assured by the gracious reception given me by Lelia, and still desirous to profit by the occasion to write her biography, I narrated little by little the history of the *fumiste*, full of stops and blunders, which she listened to with a surprising and benevolent degree of indulgence.

At last, when I thought that her image was sufficiently traced in my brain, I cut short my narrative and made a hasty exit, enchanted to be able to declare to my reader that the *St. Petersburgh Gazette* does not know what it says; and that three-fourths of those who chatter about George Sand amuse themselves at her expense. It is true that the prophetess smokes a cigar, or perhaps more than one; and that she condescends, now and then, to wear a great coat; that amongst her intimate acquaintances they call her George, for brevity; but all that is not forbidden by our laws. I would also add, if I am to believe persons that are well informed on the subject, that there are some drawing-rooms in Paris where the illustrious writer is to be seen uniting the simplicity of genius with the modest grace of woman.

Now that you know as much on the subject as I do myself, it only remains for me to tell you by what concatenation of circumstances the poetess came to purchase glory at the price of her peace of mind.

In the first year of the restoration, the aristocratical convent of the *Dames Anglaises*, situated in the *Rue des Fosses-Saint-Victor*, which entirely enjoyed the monopoly of all patrician educations, opened its doors one fine morning to a young and interesting scholar.

The new comer, who might have passed fourteen summers, came from Berry; her religious instruction seemed to have been much neglected, for the good sisters remarked, with a kind of shudder, that she persisted in making the sign of the cross in a philosophical left-handed kind of manner, which plainly denoted that she was not much in the habit of crossing herself. She was what we call a fine dark child: her marked features gave her a sort of wild fierceness; and she bore without much annoyance those uncharitable looks which are always liberally bestowed upon new comers. whether at college or at convents. There was in all her manners a rustic rudeness; so much so, that in a few days after her arrival she was named by her noble, witty companions, *the boy*. As far as regards birth and fortune, the new comer could vie in greatness with any there; for although by her father's side she only possessed opulence, yet her grandmother had royal blood in her veins, in this wise:

Every one knows, or is supposed to know, tha Marshal Saxe was the natural son of Augustus II King of Poland, and of the Countess of Kœnigs-mark. Under a Saxon outside, the hero of Fontenoy possessed a truly French heart; in his lifetime he had made a number of conquests; and the issue of one of these, in 1750, proved to be a daughter, Marie Aurore, recognised as such after the death of the Marshal by a decree in parliament. Her first mar-riage was with Count Horn; she remained a widow but for a short period. The Countess Horn retired to her country seat, *l'Abbaye-aux-Bois*, and under that predestined roof, which at a later period shel-tered a beauty immortalised by goodness and grace, she held her delightful *re-unions*, the most distin-guished of those days; the old *Maréchal de Richelieu* frequented them, and was, it seems, one of her most devoted admirers. Remarkably good-looking and witty, the young widow inspired a M. Dupin de Franceuil, son of Claude Dupin, with a feeling of love. They were soon after united; and he took her to Berry, where he was just nominated to a very valuable government appointment. Afterwards she resided successively at Chateauroux, and the Castle of Nohant, about a league from Chatre. Madame Dupin again found herself a widow, in 1786, with a son, Maurice Dupin. He married at an early age, and had just gained, under the Empire, a high military grade (he was, I think, a colonel), when he died suddenly at Chatre, of a fall from a horse, leaving an only daughter, named, like her grandmother, Marie Aurore, and whose education was confided to her care.

This child, who was to be the George Sand, was first of all brought up *à la* Jean Jacques. It was a little child in short frocks, that was allowed to play on the banks of the river Indre, and to run after butterflies in all the gardens of the chateau, and at night tired of her frolics, used to hear marvellous stories told about the pomp of the palace of Versalles; of the pleasures of *Trianon;* the mysteries of the *Parc aux Cerfs;* and about philosophers and wits of bygone times. She never forgot these tales; and it is by their aid that you are able to explain the way in which she possessed so much originality, such a florid style, so unpassioned, yet so abounding in the deepest pathos. In the *Marquise,* for instance, she goes back to the time of our ancestors, and truthfully depicts the manners, customs, passions, and mincing dialect that were so much in vogue in those days.

At the time of the religious reaction that followed the restoration, Madame Dupin thought it high time to sacrifice a portion of her philosophical method, and make room for the new ideas, and to give her grand daughter an education suitable to her position and her high birth, and the rank which her large fortune entitled her to assume in the world.

It was then that the fine but rustic child of Berry quitted the chateau to come to Paris, and entered the convent; she had been there but a few months when the alteration effected in her was wonderful. The ardent imagination that at a later period was so finely developed, began to show itself in its full force. The majesty and pomp of the Catholic reli-gion, the uniform manner of living, the tranquil and pious atmosphere of the cloister, all that produced in ner soul a complete revolution; and Mademoiselle Aurore found herself suddenly seized with such fits of fervid devotion, that even the mode of living did not seem to her strict enough, nor the rules suffi-ciently severe; so much so, that the superior often found that it was absolutely necessary to moderate her religious zeal, out of consideration for her health, and in making her feel, that destined as she was to fill a certain position in the world, she would be obliged to reduce her intemperate ardour.

Six years after that there resided in the chateau

of Nohant a woman dying of weariness and melancholy; it was the pious scholar of the convent deploring her lost liberty, and cursing the yoke that she would no doubt shortly wear. She had just left the convent when she lost her grandmother; and then alone, without counsel, without a guide, without support, young, rich, and an orphan, she had allowed herself to be united to a man after the fashion of bygone days, and only too much in vogue now. A marriage was arranged for her; one that was called by the world *suitable*. Pity the world should have a voice in such matters! Lively and susceptible as *Indiana;* candid and enthusiastic as *Valentine;* proud and stubborn as *Lelia;* she found herself united to a soldier who had retired from active service with some little fame, but the most prosaic being under heaven. Her husband was a worthy old campaigner, and a native of Aquitaine, holding refinements of the heart and mind as idle nonsense and trash, taking life for what it is worth, and time only while it lasts, not very learned, and very abrupt and ungentlemanly, if we may judge by the tenour of a law-suit that was at that period instituted against him.

The first years of this new life were tranquil, though not happy. She suffered, but she struggled valiantly against her sorrow; and calling to her aid her books, her high sense of duty, but above all the holy work where consolation is offered unto the afflicted, and for which George Sand entertained a devout and holy feeling.

In 1825, Madame Dudevant was taken by her husband to the mineral waters of the Pyrenees. The impressions of this journey, the aspect of a rugged and wild country, all that awoke the imagination of her artistic nature and her womanly heart, only rendered her monotonous and dreary life still more unbearable.

At last, after many vain struggles, after many painful scenes, the bitterness of which often pierce through more than one page of George Sand, the wife parted—the poetess took wings; and one fine day, in 1828, they were searching vainly all over the Castle of Nohant for her—she had disappeared. What had become of her ?   No one knew.

Here I find, in the notes, which I have every reason to believe correct, a deed which sufficiently paints the fluctuations of a noble soul, ardent and impatient.

In 1828, the confessor of the convent, who had always received the confessions of Mademoiselle Dupin, came one day to beg of the superior to accord him a favour. He told her that one of his penitents, an old scholar, finding herself in a painful position, wished to find in the convent a pious retreat. The superior at first refused; alleging for a reason the rules of the convent. The confessor insisted, and at last obtained his wish; and the fugitive from Nohant again crossed the door of that peaceful abode where her early years had passed away in so tranquil a manner. But her destiny called her elsewhere—genius reclaimed its prey; and a few days from that period she again appeared before the world, to encounter all the risks, all the passions, all the joys, and all the troubles of a poet's life.

The period on which we now enter is a delicate one, and one on which it is not easy to obtain facts. A biographer may be wanting in talent and wit, but he must never be deficient in dignity or truth. Above all, when he speaks of a genius, to whom blame, praise, or complaints are attached, truth must be more strictly attended to than in any other case. For those who like to hear relations, I will transcribe a page from the *Lettres d'un Voyageur.*

"I do not care about getting old; but I should not like to get old alone. I have never met the being with whom I would like to live and die; or if I have, I have never known how to retain him. Listen to an affecting story: 'There was a good artist, named Watelet, who was also a very excellent

B

wood-engraver. He loved Margaret Lecompte, and
he taught her to engrave as well as himself. She
left her husband, her wealth, and her native place,
to live with Watelet. The world at first despised
them ; and afterwards, as they were poor and unos-
tentatious, forgot them. Forty years after they were
discovered in a pretty cottage near the environs of
Paris, named the *Pretty Mill ;* the old man, still
employed at the wood-engraving, and the old woman,
known as the mistress of the mill, both sitting at
the same table.———The last engraving they had
done together represented the *Pretty Mill*, and the
house of Marguerite, with this device : *Cur valle
permutem Sabinâ divitias operosiores ?* It is framed in
my room just above another, of which nobody here
has ever seen the original. For more than a year,
the being who gave me that portrait, used to sit
with me every night, at a small table—he lived by
the same occupation as myself. At break of day
we used to compare our writings ; and we used to
sup at the little table, talking of art, sentiment,
and the future. Pray for me, oh, Marguerite
Lecompte !"

Here is another tale that has some connection with
the preceding one :

A little time after the revolution of July, a book
was published bearing the title, *Rose and Blanche ;*

or the Actor and the Nun. This book, which had but
a very poor sale at first, fell by accident into the
hands of a librarian ; he read it, and was struck by
tne fine description given to certain events, and the
novelties of the situations ; he got the address of
the writer, which was a modest furnished lodging ;
he ascended the stairs, and he there saw a young
man writing at a table, and a young woman colour-
ing artificial flowers by his side. It was Watelet
and Marguerite Lecompte. The librarian spoke of
the book ; and it turned out that Marguerite, who
understood writing works as well, if not better,
than Watelet, had written the best part of the one
in question ; only as there was no sale for them, or
if any, a very trifling one, she was obliged to colour
flowers as well, to obtain a livelihood. Encouraged
oy the praise of the librarian, she took out of a
drawer a manuscript written in her own hand-writ-
ing. The librarian examined it ; bought it for a
mere trifle, I suppose : he might have paid dearer
for it without making a bad bargain, for it was the
manuscript of *Indiana.* A short time after, Marguerite Lecompte quitted Watelet, and took a portion
of his name—George ; and from that time called
herself George Sand. From the half of his name
she has been enabled to make an entire appellation—

one that shines amongst the greatest and most glorious of the present age.

In less than ten years George Sand wrote more than thirty volumes, which the critics attacked one after another: she only wrote the faster; they attacking, she defending, her moral, philosophical, and political doctrines. All the result that seemed to arise from this controversy was, that the critic was criticising nothing, for she had begun by supposing that which never existed; they had taken as George Sand somewhere says, *bladders for lanterns:* that is to say, passions for reasons, eloquent complaints for systems, and exclamations for conclusions.

Blame as much as you will the sterile theories of art for art; blame the artist for not coming to a conclusion, or for continuing to write when he has no conclusion to arrive at, if you will; but do not make him transform himself—do not force him to come to a conclusion if it is not of his own free will: let conviction come gradually. You do not gain any way by forcing his inclinations; for if you stone him he only gains notoriety. He turns naturally against those who incense him—they do not gain by it; for violent in his conscience, the poet brings to bear on the subject so much fantastic philosophy—the worst of all philosophy. In good

truth, we take the matter too seriously with our
poets: let each one be free as air—let each man's
doctrines circulate—let us not condemn that which
we do not sufficiently understand. In religion, as
in affairs of state, let the watchword be liberty of
thought and action.

Nations that grow old, have infirmities and disagreeable ways, like old men. The Greeks of the
lower empire, for instance, were subtle and sophis-
ticated beyond measure. They were strange an-
alysts, though they did not search into everything.
Now we, that are by nature of a more inquiring
turn, lose ourselves in space. They were short-
sighted, and saw not afar off: we, on the contrary,
that view by the eye of reason, see much. But no
more about the history of the Greeks—matter of
fact history suits narrow minds; but we, we write
the philosophy of history; that is to say, that with
any person's travels in the East, we would write you
a random history of the Great Mogul, or the empire
of China, although as far as facts are concerned we
know not one word. In religion we are neither
catholics, protestants, atheists, nor deists, but we
are *pantheistes*, which is very grand, very fine, but
rather misty. In religion, as in politics, we cannot
care for the individual, or the family, or the city, or
the state; we have forsooth, something else to do.

The millions want looking after. The forest, as the German Menzel said, prevents us from seeing the individual tree. There was a time when poets made simple poetry; but now, how changed; we make social poetry. There was a time when composers composed simple melodies; but now, how changed; we have apocryphal music. There was a time when painters drew simple subjects; but now we have metaphysical painting. And I have no doubt if Dante or Shakespere were to revisit "*the gentle glimpses of the moon*," they would be astonished at hearing so many learned things of theirs brought to bear on the subject, that were written without any such intent. I had always thought that Raphael was a great painter; but I read the other day that he was the greatest theologian of the sixteenth century.

In the thickest of all this confusion, appeared a woman with all the qualities and all the faults that constitute a poet. Fervid inspiration, passionate but mobile organisation, heated imagination, a rich flow of language—nothing was wanting; not even the toilsome and painful life of an author. Unhappy in her union, she had left her marriage state: rich, she had left behind all her wealth; only reserving her liberty, which the gods, the gipsies, and the poets, will have everywhere. She could not starve—she

I new not what to do. She was advised to write, and she did write; and the profoundly philosophica or perverse thought that gave birth to her first work was the humble means, to use her own words, that also gave her bread. The book had a prodigious success; it was a tale written with feeling, and burning with passion, pain, and anger. The plot was not new; it told of a wife, a husband, and a lover. The portrait of the husband was not flattering—it would have astonished me had he been otherwise: the lover himself—and this would seem to indicate a first deception—the lover, that an eminent writer called (I do not know why) the king of all her works, cut in the tale but a very sorry and painful figure: the fine part, and that was natural enough, was for the wife. The critic that wonders at everything, was astonished at its success; and righted himself by declaring that all women have a novel in their hearts; and once on paper there's an end. Six months after, *Valentine* appeared, and gave the critic the lie. The author, not having lived long enough, had but one string to her bow: it again treated of a husband, a wife, and a lover; but the arrow was pointed in another direction. From brutal and ignorant the husband had become coldly polite, and profoundly selfish: the lover was also much improved; he had become noble, generous, and handsome; with different qualities the wife was still the same. In *Jacques*, the third novel that was written before *Lelia*, the principal characters are always the wife, the husband, and the lover: only in this one the husband has the finest part. *Jacques* has all that is necessary to make the happiness of a woman: he is grand and noble; but he has so much generosity in his soul that you cannot help loving him; the lover sees he has no chance against such a paragon of perfection. Octave is but a common melo-dramatic lover; and yet at last the husband makes way for him. It has been generally allowed that this is one of George Sand's most immoral works; they said it tended to prove that a husband's worth went for nothing in marriage. I do not know what was the author's first thought, but it seems to me, who am unbiassed on the subject, to have been this: Fernande is a little fool who likes her husband without comprehending him, and suddenly ceases liking him without knowing why, and ultimately deceives him. I do not think the book dangerous; and I do not think that there is any female who in her inmost thoughts ever condemned the book for its immorality.

After *Jacques* came *Lelia:* since *Indiana*, the author had lived, had loved, had by turns loved and ceased to be loved, had suffered, she had enlarged her sufferings with all the strength of her imagination, and all the little tortures of her doubtful position. Never having loved in her married state, she despaired of ever loving either life, God, or man, and one day in an access of intermittent fever she wrote *Lelia*.

When this book appeared, the double halo of repulsion and enthusiasm surrounded the name of George Sand; the philosophical phalanx offered her the arm, saying: Good morrow, noble prophetess! while the sticklers for propriety shook their fists, calling her *empoisonneuse!*

It was a truly poetical novel, written in a sort of delirium, which had overturned her faculties to the detriment of her reason. *Lelia* is at once her finest, yet her worst work; it is certainly the least logical of all her compositions, but all its parts are majestic and varied; there is true beauty and dignity in every passage. *Lelia, Trenmor, Sténie*, and *Pulchérie* are four living types that do not represent ideas out the true condition of the soul; these four personages discourse and discuss *ad infinitum*. Every one is wrong and right by turns; they all finish by being wrong, for the work is without end; and the reader stretches himself on his arm chair, exclaiming with the poet:

"No perfect happiness is here below."

The soul of George Sand got calmer after the
appearance of *Lelia*. Her social position too, took a
firmer stand. She was legally divorced from her
husband, re-entered in possession of her fortune,
and borrowed from the mountains of Switzerland
and the fine sky of Florence and Venice less sombre
thoughts. She there wrote two or three charming
tales, *Secretaire Intime* and *Leon Leoni*, etc. In
these two works she laid aside the everlasting wife,
husband and lover, and the mournful phraseology of
Lelia. Without being consoling, her ideas were
more purely artistical and less bitter. Afterwards
appeared *André:* that charming tale that ought to
be ranked with *Paul and Virginia*, were it not for a
certain grossness that she infused into *André*, which
seems incompatible with the whole tenor of his conduct. George Sand somewhere says: "Angels are
not more pure than the heart of a young man of
twenty, when he loves with passion." It is well
said, and it is true; for corrupted, faithless, and
almost Don Juans, as we all are, there is hardly one
of us that has not truly and earnestly loved at that
age of candour.

After *André* came *Simon Mauprat*, and the *Lettres
d'un Voyageur*, etc. etc. The period of anger gradually subsided into a calm, and into poetry and truth.
A noble friendship was established between two

souls carrying on in different spheres an equal talent. M. de Lamennais took the direction of a periodical called the *World*, and George Sand published in it her five letters addressed to *Marcia*, full of christian resignation. These letters were sufficient to reduce to naught the philosophical sentiments expressed in *Lelia*.

In all ages christianity has never been stayed for any length of time ; the adventurous and turbulent poet only crosses its peaceful lines with his arms and baggage, to enter the tent of *Pantheism*, and towards the close of his existence return to his former camp.

After a voyage to the Balearic Isles, *Spiridion* was written. This book, written under the cool shade of *Palma*, was a strange contradiction, for it reproduced all the sentiments expressed in *Lelia*. The edifice hardly raised by the *Lettres à Marcie*, found itself crumbled by *Spiridion*. And the progressive christianity of M. de Lamennais was left in the rear. Since, in a late edition of *Lelia*, and in several of the latest works of George Sand, she gets further and further from the principles of christianity, and her thoughts have taken a decided turn in favour of republicanism. Of purely artistical works, she has written several of late that I cannot analyze here.

We now see her in unexplored regions; that is, writing a drama named *Cosima*.

Now, reader, if you want this biography to conclude, I must tell you for conclusion that there is none. There is not, until now, any work of George Sands' on which to found an accusation—no one on which to rest an apology: that her works prove every thing because they prove nothing; for if there is poison on one side, you have only to turn the leaf to find the antidote. And that the impious, immoral, and anti-social notions of the past ages seem to me as absurd as the *pantheistical* doctrines of the present age.

As to the pernicious influence of her writings, I think all that much exaggerated. Nearly all her works possess at the end a sort of unhappy morality, which to a certain point replaces the other. If there are passions and faults there is also regret and remorse; and vice occurs but rarely. She also makes them stray from the right path, but she never degrades them. To read her writings, where the most opposite sentiments are expressed by one pen, you experience a painful admiration; and when you put them down, you seek for truth with more force than ever. You feel that what you have read is not the actual state of things; that imagination is not reason; and that poets will always be poets—that is to say, they are like melodious birds, any noise will make them sing. Let the noise come from within or without, let it charm or let it alarm, let it attract or let it repulse, let it be a wish just born or let it be a brook that murmurs, let it be a people that sway or the sea that roars, a throne that crumbles or an illusion that is past, they sing! ay, they will sing! ask them why they sing? they will say because they are birds!!!

ENCHANTED LAKE

CHAPTER I.

THE AUTHOR TO THE READER.

A la sueur de ton visaige
Tu gaigneras ta panvre vie.
Apres long travail et usaige,
Voicy la *mort* qui te convie.*

THIS old French couplet, inscribed beneath one o
Holbein's compositions, is deeply sad in its simpli
city. The engraving represents a husbandmar
driving his plough in the middle of a field. A vas
landscape stretches in the distance: you there see
wretched cabins; the sun is setting behind the hill.
It is the end of a day of hard work. The peasant
_s old, thick set, covered with rags. His four horses
are poor, worn out; the ploughshare buries itself in
a rough, ungrateful soil. Only one being is brisk

---

* In the sweat of thy face
Thou shalt gain thy poor life.
After labour long and wearing,
Here is *death* who invites thee !

and active in this scene of *travail et usaige*. It is a
fantastic personage, a skeleton armed with a whip,
who runs in the furrow by the side of the frightened
horses and strikes them, acting thus as a ploughboy
to the old husbandman. It is death, that spectre
which Holbien has allegorically introduced into the
succession of philosophical and religious subjects, at
once gloomy and ludicrous, entitled *The Shadows of
Death*.

In that collection, or rather in that vast composition in which death, playing his part on every page,
is the tie and the predominant thought, Holbien has
brought upon the stage the sovereigns, the pontiffs,
the gamblers, the drunkards, the nuns, the courte-
sans, the brigands, the poor, the warriors, the monks,
the Jews, the travellers, all the world of his time
and of our own; and everywhere the spectre of
death mocks, threatens, triumphs. From one picture only is it absent. It is that in which poor
Lazarus, lying upon a dunghill at the door of the
rich man, declares that he does not fear it, doubtless
because he has nothing to lose, and because his life
is an anticipated death.

Is this stoical thought of the half-pagan Christianity of the restoration very consoling? and do
religious minds find it for their advantage? The
ambitious man, the cheat, the tyrant, the debauchee,
all those proud sinners who abuse life, and whom
death holds by the hair, will be punished, without
doubt; but the blind man, the beggar, the crazy
man, the poor peasant, are they compensated for

their long misery by the simple reflection that death is not an evil to them? No, an implacable sadness, a horrible fatality weighs upon the work of the artist. It resembles a bitter curse cast upon the lot of humanity.

It was indeed the sorrowful satire, the true picture of society which Holbein had before his eyes. Crime and wretchedness,—this was what struck him; but we, artists of another age, what shall we paint? Shall we seek in the thought of death for the remuneration of our present humanity? Shall we invoke it as the punishment of injustice and the compensation of suffering? No, we have now nothing to do with death, but everything with life. We no longer believe, either in the nothingness of the tomb, or in the salvation purchased by a forced renunciation; we wish that life should be good, because we wish it to be fruitful. Lazarus must leave his dunghill, in order that the poor may no longer rejoice at the death of the rich. All must be happy, in order that the happiness of a few may not be criminal and cursed in the sight of God. The husbandman in sowing his grain, must know that he labours at the work of life, and not rejoice because death walks by his side. Finally, death must no longer be the punishment of prosperity, nor the consolation of distress. God has not destined it either to punish or to compensate for life, and the grave should not be a refuge to which it is lawful to refer those whom we do not wish to make happy.

Certain artists of our age, casting a serious glance

upon that which surrounds them, apply themselves
to depict the sorrows, the abjectness of poverty, the
dunghill of Lazarus.   This may be the domain of
art and of philosophy; but in depicting poverty so
ugly, so debased, sometimes so vicious and so criminal, is their object attained, and is the effect salutary,
as they would wish?   We dare not decide upon this
point.   It may be said that by displaying the abyss
excavated beneath the fragile soil of opulence, they
terrify the wicked rich man, as in the time of the
Dance of Macaber* they showed him the yawning
grave, and death ready to entwine him with its un-
clean arms.   In our day they show him the thief
picking the lock of his door, and the assassin watching his slumbers.   We confess that we do not understand too well how he will be reconciled with the
humanity which he despises, how he will be made
to feel for the sufferings of the poor man whom he
fears, by showing him that poor man under the form
of an escaped convict and of a night prowler.   The
horrid death grinning its teeth and playing upon the
violin in the pictures of Holbein and his predeces-
sors, did not find the means, under this aspect, of
converting the wicked and consoling the victims.
Does not our literature proceed in this matter somewhat in the style of the artists of the middle ages
and of the restoration?

Holbein's drinkers fill their cups with a kind of

* Holbein is said to have derived the idea of his "Dance of
Death" from this composition.

fury, in order to drive away the idea of death, who,
invisible to them, serves them as cup-bearer. The
rich of our day ask for fortifications and cannons, in
order to drive away the idea of the insurgent popu-
lace, whom art displays to them working in the dark,
in detail, while awaiting the propitious moment for
destroying social order. The church of the middle
ages replied to the terrors of the powerful by the
sale of indulgences; the governments of our age
calm the anxieties of the rich by making them pay
for a great many gend'armes and jailors, bayonets
and prisons.

Albert Durer, Michael Angelo, Holbein, Callot,
and Goya made powerful satires on the evils of their
age and country. These are immortal works, his-
torical pages of incontestable value; we do not wish
to deny to artists the right of probing the wounds
of society, and placing them before our eyes; but is
there nothing to be accomplished now except to depict terror and threatening? In that literature of
the mysteries of iniquity, which talent and imagination have brought into fashion, we prefer the sweet
and gentle figures to the criminals with their dra-
matic effects. The former may undertake and bring
about conversions, the latter produce fear, and fear
does not cure selfishness, but augments it.

We believe that the mission of art is a mission of
feeling and of love; that the novel of our day ought
to replace the parables and apologues of simpler
times, and that the artist has a task more broad and
more poetical than that of proposing a few measures

of prudence and conciliation to diminish the fear inspired by his paintings. His aim ought to be to cause the objects of his solicitude to be loved, and, in case of need, I would not make it a crime in him to embellish them somewhat. Art is not a study of positive reality; it is a search after ideal truth, and the *Vicar of Wakefield* is a more useful book, and one more healthy to the mind than *le Paysan perverti*, or *les Liaisons dangereuses*.

Reader, forgive these observations, and please to accept them in the manner of a preface. There will be none in the little story I am about to relate to you, and it will be so short and so simple that it was necessary I should make an excuse for it beforehand by telling you what I think of terrible stories.

It is with reference to a husbandman that I have allowed myself to be led into this digression. It is in fact the story of a husbandman which I intended to tell you, and which I will tell you immediately.

I had been looking for a long while, and with a feeling of deep melancholy at Holbein's husbandman, and I was walking in the fields, dreaming of country life and the destiny of the tillers of the soil. Doubtless it is gloomy to wear out one's strength and one's days in cleaving the bosom of that jealous earth, which obliges us to force from it the treasures of its fertility, when a crust of the hardest and blackest bread is, at the end of the day, the only recompense and the only profit granted to a labour so severe. Those riches which cover the soil, those harvests, those fruits, those proud animals, which fatten in the long grass, are the property of a few, and the instruments of fatigue and slavery to the greater number. The man of leisure does not generally love for themselves, either the fields, or the meadows, or the spectacle of nature, or the superb animals which are to be converted into pieces of gold for his use. The man of leisure comes to seek a little air and health at his country residence, then he returns to spend in the great cities the proceeds of his vassals' labour.

On his side, the working man is too much exhausted, too unhappy, and too fearful of the future, to enjoy the beauties of the country and the charms of a rustic life. To him also the golden fields, the beautiful meadows, the superb animals, represent sacks of crowns of which he will have but a small portion, insufficient for his wants, and which cursed sacks he must nevertheless fill every year, in order to satisfy his master, and pay for the right to live parsimoniously and wretchedly on his domain.

And yet, nature is eternally young, beautiful and generous. She pours forth poetry and beauty to all the beings, to all the plants which are allowed to develop themselves freely in her bosom. She possesses the secret of happiness, and no one has ever known how to wrest it from her. The most happy of men would be he who, possessing the science of his labour, and working with his hands, finding comfort and liberty in the exercise of his intelligent strength, would have time to live by his heart and by his brain, to understand his own work and to love that of God. The artist has delights of this kind in the contemplation and reproduction of the beauties of nature; but, on seeing the sufferings of the men who people this paradise of the earth, the artist with an upright and humane heart is disturbed in the midst of his delight. Happiness will be there, where the mind, the heart and the hand labouring in concert under the eye of Providence, a holy harmony would exist between the munificence of God and the transports of the human soul. Then, instead of piteous and frightful death walking in the husbandman's furrow, whip in hand, the allegorical painter could place by his side a radient angel sowing with full hand the blessed wheat upon the steaming furrow.

And the dream of a sweet, free, poetical, industrious, and simple life for the man of the fields is not so difficult to be conceived that it must of necessity be classed among chimeras. Those sweet and sad words of Virgil: "O happy the man of the fields, did he but know his happiness!" are a regret; but like all regrets, they are also a prediction. A day will come when the husbandman can also be an artist, if not to express (which will be of little consequence then), at least to feel, the beautiful. Do men believe that this mysterious intuition of poetry is not already in him in the state of instinct and vague reverie? Among those whom a small inheritance protects in our day, and in whom the excess of misfortune does not smother every moral and intellectual development, pure, felt and appreciated happiness is in an elementary state; and, moreover, if from the depths of suffering and fatigue some poets' voices have already arisen, why should it be said that the labour of the hands excludes the functions of the soul? Doubtless that exclusion is the general result of excessive labour and of deep poverty; but let no one say that when man shall labour moderately and usefully, there will be only inferior workmen and inferior poets. He who derives noble delights from the feeling of poetry is a real poet, even if he have never made a verse in his life.

My thoughts had taken this direction, and I did not perceive that this confidence in the educability of the rustic man was strengthened in me by external influences. I was walking on the border of a field which some peasants were in the act of preparing for the approaching seed time. The arena was vast like that of Holbein's picture; the landscape was vast also, and enclosed with great lines of verdure, somewhat reddened by the approach of autumn, that broad field of a vigorous brown, where recent rains had left, in some furrows, lines of water which the sun made glitter like fine threads of silver. The day had been clear and warm, and the earth, freshly opened by the cutting of the ploughshares, exhaled a light vapour. In the upper part of the field, an old man, whose broad back and severe face reminded me of the one in Holbein's picture, but whose garments did not indicate poverty, gravely held his plough of antique form, drawn by two quiet oxen, with pale yellow skins, real patriarchs of the mea-

dow, large in stature, rather thin, with long turned
down horns, old labourers whom long habit had
made *brothers*, as they are called by our country
people, and who, when separated from each other,
refuse to work with a new companion, and let themselves die of sorrow. Those persons who know
nothing of the country treat as fabulous the friendship of the ox for his yoke-fellow. Let them come
and see in the depths of the stable a poor animal,
thin, drawn up, lashing his fleshless sides with un-
quiet tail, blowing with fear and disdain upon the
food that is offered him, with his eyes always turned
towards the door, or pawing with his foot the empty
place at his side, smelling of the yoke and chain
which his companion has worn, and incessantly calling him with melancholy lowings. The neat-herd
will say: "There is a yoke of oxen lost: his brother
is dead, and this one won't work any more. We
ought to be able to fat him for beef; but he won't
eat, and soon he will starve to death."

The old husbandman worked slowly, in silence,
without useless efforts; his docile team did not
hurry any more than he; but, owing to the con-
tinuity of a labour without distraction, and the ap-
pliance of tried and well sustained strength, his
furrow was as soon turned as that of his son, who
was ploughing at a short distance from him, with
four oxen not so stout, in a vein of stronger and
more stony soil.

But that which afterwards attracted my attention
was really a beautiful spectacle, a noble subject for

a painter. At the other extremity of the arable
field, a good looking young man was driving a mag-
nificent team: four pairs of young animals of a dark
colour, a mixture of black and bay with streaks of
fire, with those short and frizzly heads which still
savour of the wild bull, those large savage eyes,
those sudden motions, that nervous and jerking labour which still is irritated by the yoke and the
goad, and only obeys with a start of anger the re-
cently imposed authority. They were what are
called newly-yoked steers. The man who governed
them had to clear a corner formerly devoted to pas-
turage, and filled with century-old stumps, the task
of an athlete, for which his energy, his youth, and
his eight almost unbroken animals were barely
sufficient.

A child six or seven years old, beautiful as an
angel, with his shoulders covered, over his blouse,
by a lamb-skin, which made him resemble the little
Saint John the Baptists of the painters of the restoration, walked in the furrow parallel to the plough,
and touched the flank of the oxen with a long and
light stick pointed with a slightly sharpened goad.
The proud animals quivered under the small hand
of the child, and made their yokes and the thongs
bound over their foreheads creak, while they gave
violent shocks to the plough handles. When a root
stopped the ploughshare, the husbandman shouted
with a powerful voice, calling each beast by his
name, but rather to calm than to excite; for the
oxen, irritated by this sudden resistance, leaped, dug

up the ground with their broad forked feet, and
would have cast themselves out of the track, carrying
the plough across the field, if, with his voice and
goad, the young man had not restrained the four
nearest him, while the child governed the other
four.   He also shouted, the poor little fellow, with
a voice which he wished to make terrible, but which
remained as gentle as his angelic face.   It was all
beautiful in strength or in grace, the landscape, the
man, the child, the bulls under the yoke; and in
spite of this powerful struggle in which the earth
was overcome, there was a feeling of gentleness and
deep calm which rested upon all things.   When the
obstacle was surmounted, and the team had resumed
its equal and solemn step, the husbandman, whose
feigned violence was only an exercise of vigour and
an expenditure of activity, immediately recovered
the serenity of simple souls, and cast a look of paternal satisfaction on his child, who turned to smile
on him.   Then the manly voice of this young father
of a family struck up the melancholy and solemn
strain which the ancient tradition of the country
transmits, not to all ploughmen indiscriminately, but
to those most consummate in the art of exciting and
sustaining the ardour of the oxen at work.   This
chant, the origin of which was perhaps considered
sacred, and to which mysterious influences must
formerly have been attributed, is still reputed, at
this day, to possess the virtue of keeping up the courage of the animals, of appeasing their dissatisfaction,
and of charming the ennui of their long task.   It is

not enough to know how to drive them well while
tracing a perfectly straight furrow, to lighten their
labour by raising or depressing the point of the
ploughshare opportunely in the soil: no one is a perfect ploughman if he does not know how to sing to
the oxen, and this is a science apart, which requires
taste and peculiar adaptation.

This chant is, to say the truth, only a kind of
recitative, interrupted and resumed at will. Its
irregular form and its false intonations, speaking
according to the rules of musical art, render it un-
translatable. But it is none the less a beautiful
chant, and so appropriate to the nature of the labour
which it accompanies, to the gait of the ox, to the
calmness of those rural scenes, to the simplicity of
the men who sing it, that no genius, a stranger to
the labours of the soil, could have invented it, and
no singer other than a *finished ploughman* of that
country could repeat it. At those epochs of the
year when there is no other labour and no other
movement in the country than that of ploughing,
this chant, so simple and so powerful, rises like a
voice of the breeze, to which its peculiar toning gives
it a kind of resemblance. The final note of each
phrase, continued and trilled with an incredible
length and power of breath, ascends a quarter of a
note with systematic dissonance. This is wild, but
the charm of it is invincible, and when you become
accustomed to hear it, you cannot conceive how any
song could be sung at those hours and in those places
without disturbing their harmony.

It therefore happened that I had under my eyes a picture which contrasted with Holbein's, though the scene was a parallel one. Instead of a sad old man, a young and active one; instead of a team of panting and harrassed horses, a double quadriga of stout and ardent oxen; instead of death, a beautiful child; instead of an image of despair and destruction, a spectacle of energy and a thought of happiness.

It was then that the French couplet

A la sueur de ton visaige, &c.,

and the "*O fortunatos . . . agricolas*" of Virgil, came together to my mind; and, that on seeing this beautiful pair, the man and the child, accomplish under such poetical conditions, and with so much gracefulness united with strength, a labour full of grandeur and solemnity, I felt a deep pity mingled with an involuntary respect. Happy the husbandman! Yes, doubtless, I should be happy in his place, if my arm, suddenly become strong, and my chest become powerful, could thus fertilize and sing nature, without my eyes ceasing to see and my brain to comprehend the harmony of colours and of sounds, the fineness of tones, and the gracefulness of outlines—in one word, the mysterious beauty of things! and especially without my heart ceasing to be in relation with the divine feeling which presided over the immortal and sublime creation!

But, alas! that man has never understood the mystery of the beautiful, that child will never understand it. May God preserve me from believing that they are not superior to the animals they govern, and that they have not at moments a kind of ecstatic revelation which charms their fatigue and soothes their cares! I see upon their noble foreheads the seal of the Lord, for they are born kings of the soil, much more than those who own it because they have paid for it. And the proof that they feel this is, that they cannot be expatriated with impunity, that they love this soil watered with their sweat, that the true peasant dies of nostalgia under the harness of the soldier, far from the field that saw his birth. But this man wants a part of the delights that I possess, immaterial delights which are certainly his right, his, the workman of this vast temple, which heaven alone is vast enough to enclose. He wants the knowledge of his feelings. Those who have condemned him to servitude from his mother's womb, not being able to deprive him of revery, have deprived him of reflection.

Well! such as he is, incomplete and condemned to an eternal childhood, he is much more beautiful than he in whom science has smothered feeling. Do not elevate yourselves above him, you who think yourselves invested with the legitimate and imprescriptive right to command him, for this frightful error under which you labour proves that your mind has killed your heart, and that you are the most incomplete and the blindest of men. I love the simplicity of his soul still more than the false lights of yours, and if I had to relate his life, I should have more pleasure in bringing forward its sweet and touching points than you would have merit in depicting the abjectness into which the rigours and the contempt of your social precepts may have precipitated him.

I was acquainted with that young man and with that beautiful child. I knew their history. For they had a history—every one has a history, and each might be interested in the romance of his own life, if he had comprehended it. Although a peasant and simple ploughman, Germain had reflected upon his duties and his affections. He had related them to me with simplicity and clearness, and I had listened to him with interest. When I had beer looking at him a long while as he ploughed, I asked myself why his history should not be written, although it was a history as simple, as straight, and as devoid of ornament as the furrow he was turning with his plough.

Next year that furrow will be filled up and covered by a new one. Thus also is impressed and disappears the trace of the greater portion of mankind in the field of humanity. A little earth effaces it, and the furrows we have opened follow each other like the graves in a cemetery. Is not the furrow of the ploughman quite as valuable as that of the idle man, who has nevertheless a name, a name which will survive, if by singularity or any absurdity he makes a little noise in the world?

Well! let us save, if we can, from the nothingness of oblivion, the furrow of Germain, the *finished husbandman*. He will know nothing about it and will not care; but I shall have had some pleasure in attempting it.

CHAPTER II.

GERMAIN THE FINISHED PLOUGHMAN.

"GERMAIN," said his father-in-law to him one day,
" you must nevertheless decide upon taking another
wife. It will soon be two years since my daughter
died, and your eldest boy is seven years old. You
are almost thirty, my son, and you know that when
past that age, in our country, a man is considered
too old to marry again. You have three beautiful
children, and hitherto they have not been any trouble to us. My wife and my daughter-in-law have
taken care of them in the best way they could, and
have loved them as they ought. Now, Petit-Pierre
is almost brought up; he drives the oxen quite
cleverly, he is steady enough to watch the cattle in
the meadow, and strong enough to lead the horses
to water. Therefore we need not be troubled about
him; but the two others—whom we love nevertheless, God knows, the poor innocents! give us a good
deal of anxiety this year. My daughter-in-law is
quite near her confinement, and she still has a very
small child in her arms. When the one we expect
shall come, she will no longer be able to take care of
your little Solange, and especially of your Sylvian,
who is not yet four years old, and who is never quiet
day nor night. He has quick blood, like yourself;

that will make a good workman, but it makes a terrible child ; and my old woman can't run fast enough
now to catch him when he steals off to the side of
the ditch, or when he throws himself under the feet
of the cattle. And besides, with this other that my
daughter-in-law is about to bring into the world, her
next youngest will fall for a year at least upon my
wife s hands. Therefore your children trouble us
and overtask us. We do not like to see children
badly tended ? and when we think of the accidents
that may happen to them for want of watching, we
have no peace or comfort. Therefore you must have
another wife and I another daughter-in-law. Think
about it, my boy. I have already warned you frequently, time flies, the years will not wait for you.
You owe to your children, and to us, who wish
everything to go on well in the house, that you
marry again as soon as possible."

" Very well, father," said the son-in-law, "if you
really desire it, I must satisfy you. But I cannot
conceal from you that it will grieve me a great deal,
and that I have no more wish to do it than to drown
myself. We know what we lose and we do not know
what we find. I had an honest wife, a handsome
wife ; gentle, courageous, good to her father and
mother, good to her husband, good to her children,
good for labour in the fields as well as in the house,
skilful in her work, good for everything in fine ; and
when you gave her to me, when I took her, we did
not make it a condition that I should succeed in forgetting her if I had the misfortune to lose her."

D

"What you say comes from a good heart, Germain," replied father Maurice; "and I know that you loved my daughter, that you made her happy, and that if you could have satisfied death by taking her place, Catherine would be alive at this hour, and you in the cemetery. She really deserved to be loved so much by you, and if you are not consoled for her loss, neither are we consoled. But I do not ask you to forget her. The good God has willed that she should leave us, and we shall not pass a day without letting her know by our prayers, our thoughts, our words and our actions, that we respect her remembrance and that we are grieved for her departure. But if she could speak to you from the other world, and let you know her wishes, she would command you to seek a mother for her poor little orphans. The question therefore is to find a woman worthy to take her place. That will not be very easy; but it is not impossible; and when we shall have found her for you, you will love her as you loved my daughter, because you are an honest man, and because you will feel obliged to her for doing us a service, and for loving your children."

"It is well, father Maurice," replied Germain; "I will do your will, as I have always done it."

"It is but justice to you to acknowledge, my son, that you have always listened to the friendship and good reasons of the head of your family. Let us consult together, therefore, about the choice of your new wife. In the first place, I am not of opinion that you had better take a young person. That is not what you want. Youth is flighty : and as it is a burden to bring up three children, especially when they belong to another woman, it requires a good soul, very steady, very gentle, and well inclined to work. If your wife is not about the same age with you, she will not have reason enough to accept such a duty. She will consider you too old and your children too young. She will complain and your children will suffer."

"That is exactly what makes me anxious," said Germain. "If those poor little ones should come to be maltreated, hated, beaten !"

"God forbid!" returned the old man. "But wicked women are more rare in our country than good ones, and we must be very stupid not to find such a one as would suit our purpose."

"That is true, father ; there are good girls in our village ; there is Louise, Sylvaine, Claudine, Marguerite—in fine, any one you choose."

"Gently, gently, my boy, all those girls are too young, or too poor—or too pretty ; for really we must think of that also, my son. A pretty woman is not always as steady as another."

"Do you then wish me to take an ugly one ?" said Germain, a little troubled.

"No! not ugly, by any means ; for this woman will bring you other children, and there is nothing so sad as to have ugly, mean-looking, or unhealthy children. But a woman, still fresh, with good health, and who is neither handsome nor ugly, would be just what you want."

"I see plainly," said Germain, smiling rather sadly, "that, to have her such as you wish, it would be necessary to make her on purpose; and the more because you do not wish her to be poor, and the rich ones are not easy to be had, especially for a widower."

"And if she were a widow herself, Germain? For instance, a widow without children and with a handsome property?"

"I don't know of any such at this moment in our parish."

"Nor I either, but there are such elsewhere."

"You have some one in view, father; then tell me at once."

"Yes, I have one in view: it is one Leonard, Guerin's widow, who lives at Fourche."

"I know neither the woman nor the place," replied Germain, resigned, but more and more sad.

"Her name is Catherine, the same as your dead wife."

"Catherine? Yes, it would give me pleasure to have to say that name; Catherine! And yet, if I cannot love her as well as the other, that will give me still more pain; it will remind me of her more frequently."

"I tell you that you will love her; she is a good person, a woman of great heart; I have not seen her for a long while; she was not an ugly girl then; but she is no longer young; she is thirty-two years old. She is of a good family, all honest people, and she owns eight or ten thousand francs in land, which she would willingly sell, in order to buy other land in the place where she should be established; for she also thinks of marrying again, and I know that if your character suits her, she would not consider your position unfavourable."

"Then you have already arranged that?"

"Yes, allowing for the consent of both of you; and that is what you must ask each other when you become acquainted. The father of this woman is distantly related to me, and he has been a great friend of mine. You know father Leonard very well?"

"Yes, I have seen him talking with you at the fairs; and, at the last one, you breakfasted together; then that was what you talked about so long?"

"Without doubt; he was looking at you as you sold your cattle, and he thought you went about it well, that you were a good-looking youth, that you appeared active and understanding; and when I had told him all that you are, and how well you behave with us, during the eight years that we live and work together, without our ever having had a troublesome or angry word, he took it into his head to make you marry his daughter; which is agreeable to me also, I confess to you, from the good reputation she has, from the honesty of her family, and the good condition of her property."

"I see, father Maurice, that you think a good deal about the property."

"Without doubt, I do think a good deal about it And do not you also?'

"Yes, I do, it you wish, to give you pleasure; but you know that, for my part, I never trouble myself about what comes to me, or does not come to me, in our profits. I do not understand anything about making divisions, and my head is not good for such matters. I am well acquainted with the soil, with oxen, horses, teaming, seeding, threshing, foddering. As to sheep, vines, gardening, the small profits, and nicer cultivation, you know that is your son's business, and that I do not interfere much in it. As to money, my memory is short, and I should prefer giving up everything rather than dispute about mine and thine. I should fear to be mistaken, and to claim what did not belong to me; and if the business were not very simple and clear, I could never make my way through it."

"So much the worse, my son; and this is why I should wish you to have a wife of some head to replace me when I shall be here no longer. You have never been willing to look carefully into our accounts, and that might occasion some disagreement between you and my son, when you no longer have me to keep you in harmony, and to tell you what belongs to each."

"May you live a long while, father Maurice! But do not be disturbed about what will happen after you. I shall never dispute with your son. I confide in Jacques as much as in yourself; and as I have no property of my own, since all that may fall to me comes from your daughter, and belongs to our children, I may well be easy, and you also. Jacques would not wish to rob his sister's children for the sake of his own, since he loves the first almost as well as the last."

"You are right in that, Germain. Jacques is a good son, a good brother, and a man who loves the truth. But Jacques may die before your children are grown up, and we must always think in a family not to leave minors without a head to advise them well and to arrange their difficulties; otherwise the lawyer folks interfere, make them quarrel together, and consume everything in lawsuits. Thus, therefore, we must not think of introducing among us an additional person, whether man or woman, without saying to ourselves that some day that person may perhaps have to direct the conduct and the business of some thirty children, grandchildren, sons-in-law, and daughters-in-law—we don't know how much a family may increase; and when the hive is full, and must swarm, each thinks of carrying off his honey. When I took you for my son-in-law, although my daughter was rich, and you were poor, I never reproached her for having chosen you. I saw that you were a good workman, and I knew very well that the best riches for country people like ourselves are a pair of arms and a heart like yours. When a man brings that into a family, he brings enough. But a woman! that is different; her labour in the house is good to preserve, but not to acquire. Besides, now that you are a father, and are looking for another wife, you must remember that your new children, having nothing to expect in the inheritance of those

of your first wife, would find themselves in poverty
if you should happen to die, unless your wife should
have some property on her side.   And then, the
children with whom you will increase our colony
will cost something to feed.   If this should fall on
us alone, we would feed them, very certainly, and
without complaining; but the well-being of all the
family would be diminished by it, and the first
children would have their share in the privations
occasioned by this.   When families increase beyond
measure, without the property increasing in propor-
tion, poverty comes, whatever courage they may
display.   This is what I have to say, Germain; reflect upon it, and try to make yourself agreeable to
the widow Guerin; for her good conduct and her
purse will bring here assistance in the present, and
quiet in the future."

"It is enough, father.   I will try to please her,
and to be pleased with her."

"For that purpose you must see her, and go to
visit her."

"In her village?   At Fourche?   It is some way
from here, is it not? and we have no time to be running about at this season."

"When a man is thinking about a love marriage,
he must expect to lose some time; but when it is a
marriage of reason between two persons who have
no caprices and who know what they want, it is
quickly settled.   To-morrow is Saturday, you will
make your day's work rather short, you will start
about two hours after dinner, and you will be at

Fourche by night; the moon is large now, the roads are good, and the distance is not more than three leagues. It is near Magnier. Besides, you will take the mare."

"I should like quite as well to go on foot in this fresh weather."

"Yes, but the mare is handsome, and a suitor who arrives so well mounted has a better appearance. You will put on your new clothes, and you will carry a pretty present of game to father Leonard. You will arrive as if from me, you will talk with him, you will pass the whole Sunday with his daughter, and you will come back with a yes or no on Monday morning."

"I understand," replied Germain quietly.

And yet he was not entirely easy. Germain had always been steady, as are industrious peasants. Married at twenty, he had loved but one woman in his life, and since his widowhood, though he was of an impetuous and cheerful disposition, he had not laughed or romped with any other. He had faithfully borne a real regret in his heart, and it was not without fear and without sadness that he yielded to his father-in-law; but the father-in-law had always governed the family wisely; and Germain, who had devoted himself entirely to the common work, and consequently to him who personified it, to the father of the family, Germain did not understand how he could rebel against good reasons, against the interest of all.

Nevertheless, he was sad. Few days passed that

he did not weep for his wife in secret, and though
solitude began to weigh upon him, he was more
frightened at the idea of forming a new union than
desirous to withdraw himself from his grief He
vaguely said to himself that love might console by
coming to surprise him, for love does not console
otherwise: we do not find it when we seek for it.
It comes to us when we do not expect it. This cold
project of a marriage which father Maurice presented
to him, this unknown bride, perhaps even all the
good that was told him of her reason and virtue,
gave him subject for thought. And he went along
thinking, as men think who have not ideas enough
to contend among themselves, that is, not shaping to
himself fine reasons of resistance and selfishness, but
suffering with a dull sorrow and not struggling
against an evil which it was necessary to accept.

Still father Maurice had returned to the farm-
house, while Germain, between sunset and dark,
employed the last hour of the day in stopping the
gaps which the sheep had made in the fence of an
enclosure near the buildings. He raised the thorn
bushes and propped them up with clods of earth,
while the thrushes chattered in the neighbouring
thicket, and seemed to call to him to make haste,
curious as they were to come and examine his work
as soon as he should be gone.

CHAPTER III.

PETIT-PIERRE.

FATHER MAURICE found in his house an old neighbour who had come to chat with his wife while she got a brand wherewith to light her fire. Mother Guillette lived in a very poor hut about two gunshots from the farm. But she was a woman of order and good-will. Her poor house was neat and well kept; and her garments, pieced with care, indicated respect for herself in the midst of her distress.

"You have come to get your evening fire, mother Guillette," said the old man to her. "Do you wish for anything else?"

"No, father Maurice," replied she, "nothing at present. I am not a beggar, as you know, and I do not abuse the goodness of my friends."

"That is the truth; and therefore your friends are always ready to do you service."

"I was talking with your wife, and was asking her if Germain had decided upon marrying again."

"You are not a babbler," replied father Maurice, "people can talk before you without fearing scandal: —therefore I will tell my wife and you that Germain has entire.y decided; he starts to-morrow for the domain of Fourche."

"Well and good!" cried mother Maurice; "the poor child: God grant that he may find a wife as good and as honest as himself!"

"Ah! he is going to Fourche?" observed Guillette. "Think how it happens! that is very lucky for me, and since you asked me just now if I wanted anything, I will now tell you, father Maurice, how you can oblige me."

"Say, say; we are at your service."

"I would wish that Germain would take the trouble to carry my daughter with him."

"Where then? to Fourche?"

"No, not to Fourche, but to Ormeaux, where she is going to live the rest of the year."

"How," said mother Maurice, "are you going to part with your daughter?"

"It is really necessary that she should go to service and should earn something. That grieves me greatly, and her also, poor soul! We could not make up our minds to leave each other at the epoch of the Saint John. But now Saint Martin is coming, and she has found a good place as a shepherdess in the farms of Ormeaux. The farmer passed this way the other day, as he was returning from the fair. He saw my little Marie keeping her three sheep upon the common. 'You are not very busy, my little girl,' was what he said to her; 'and three sheep for a *pastoure* are not a great many. Do you wish to have charge of a hundred? I will hire you

The shepherdess at our house has fallen sick, she is going home, and if you will come to us within a week, you shall have fifty francs for the rest of the year until the Saint John.' The child refused, but she could not help thinking about it, and telling me of it, when she came home at night, because she saw that I was sad and troubled about getting through the winter, which will be a long and hard one, since we have seen the cranes and wild geese go over a full month earlier than usual, this year. We both of us cried; but at last we took courage: we said to each other that we could not remain together, because our little patch of land produces hardly enough for one person to live on; and since Marie is so old (she is now almost sixteen), she must needs do like the others, she must earn her bread, and help her poor mother."

"Mother Guillette," said the old husbandman, "if it required only fifty francs to console you in your troubles, and to relieve you from the necessity of sending your child away from you, really, I would put you in a way of finding them, although fifty francs is a good deal for people like ourselves. But in all things we must take counsel of reason as much as of friendship. If you should be saved from the suffering of this winter, you would not be saved from the suffering to come; and the longer your daughter delays making up her mind, the more pain you and she will have in parting with each other. Little Marie is growing large and strong; and she

has not enough to do in your house. She migh
there get a habit of idleness.—'

"Oh! as to that, I have no fear of it," said Guillette. "Marie is as courageous as a girl who was
rich and at the head of a great deal of work could
be. She does not stand a minute with her arms
folded; and when we have no work on hand, she
cleans and rubs our poor furniture till she makes it
shine like a looking-glass. She is a girl that is worth
her weight in gold; and I should have greatly preferred that she should have entered as a shepherdess
with you, than go so far to serve persons whom I do
not know. You would have taken her at the Saint
John, if we could have made up our mind; but now
you have hired all your people, and we must not
think of it until the Saint John of another year."

"And I consent to it with all my heart, Guillette!
It will give me pleasure. But, in the meanwhile,
she will do well to learn her business, and accustom
herself to serve others."

"Yes, yes, without doubt; the lot is already cast.
The farmer of Ormeaux has sent to ask for her
again this morning; we have said yes; and she
must really go. But the poor child does not know
the road, and I should not like to send her so far
entirely alone. Since your son-in-law is going to
Fourche to-morrow, he can very easily take her with
him. It seems that it is quite near the domain
where she is going; that is what they tell me, for I
have never made the journey."

"It is quite near, and my son-in-law will shew

Marie was too young and too poor a child for him to think of her in that light; and unless he were a man *without heart* and *a bad man*, it was impossible he should have a culpable thought respecting her. Father Maurice was therefore in no way anxious about him when he saw him take that pretty girl behind him on horseback; and Guillette would have thought she insulted him if she had asked him to respect her as his sister. Marie took her seat upon the mare weeping, after having kissed her mother and her young friends twenty times. Germain, who was sad on his own account, pitied her sorrow so much the more, and departed with a serious air, while the people of the neighbourhood waved their hands in farewell to poor Marie, without thought of evil.

The Grise was young, handsome, and vigorous. She carried her double burden without effort, putting back her ears and champing her bit, like a proud and courageous mare as she was. On passing beside the long pasture, she perceived her mother, who was called the old Grise, as she was called the young Grise, and whinnied in token of farewell. The old Grise came to the hedge, making her shoes clatter, tried to gallop along the border of the field to follow her daughter, then, seeing her take a long trot, she whinnied in her turn, and remained pensive, uneasy, with her nose in the air, and her mouth full of grass, which she no longer thought of eating.

"That poor beast always knows her offspring," said Germain, in order to distract little Marie from

her the way. It is but right he should do so; he
will even be able to take her up behind him on the
mare, which will save her shoes. Here he is, coming
in to supper. Tell me, Germain, mother Guillette's
little Marie is going as a shepherdess to Ormeaux:
you will take her behind you on horseback, will you
not?"

"It is well," replied Germain, who was thought-
ful, but always ready to do service for his neighbours.

In our own world, such a thing would not enter
into the thought of a mother as to intrust a girl of
sixteen to the care of a man of twenty-eight! for
Germain was in reality only twenty-eight years old;
and though, according to the ideas of his country,
he was considered old in a marrying point of view,
he was still the handsomest man of the region. Labour had not yet furrowed and worn him like the
greater number of the peasants who have ten years'
work upon their heads. He was strong enough to
work ten years more without appearing old, and it
was necessary that the prejudice of age should be
very strong in the mind of a young girl to prevent
her from seeing that Germain had a fresh colour, an
eye bright and blue as the sky in May, a rosy mouth,
superb teeth, a body elegant and supple as that of a
young horse that has not yet left the pasture.

But chastity of morals is a sacred tradition in certain districts removed from the corrupting influences
of great cities, and, among all the families of Belair,
Maurice's family was reputed honest and as serving
the truth. Germain was going to seek a wife;

ner sorrow. "That makes me remember that I did not kiss my little Pierre before setting out. The naughty child was not there. He wanted, last evening, to make me promise to take him with me, and he cried an hour in his bed. This morning, again, he tried everything to persuade me. Ah! what a knowing little wheedler he is! but when he saw that it could not be, the gentleman got vexed; he ran off into the fields, and I have not seen him the whole day."

"I saw him," said little Marie, making an exertion to restrain her tears. He was running with the Soulas children along the edge of the mowing, and I felt pretty sure he had been some time away from the house, for he was hungry and was eating the wild plums and the mulberries of the thicket. I gave him the bread I had for my luncheon, and he said to me: 'Thank you, my darling Marie; when you come to our house, I will give you some biscuit.' That child of yours is too cunning, Germain."

"Yes, he is cunning," returned the husbandman; "and I don't know what I would not do for him. If his grandmother had not had more reason than I, I should not have been able to hold out about taking him, when I saw him cry so hard that his little heart was almost bursting."

"Well, why should you not have taken him, Germain? He would not have troubled you at all; he's so reasonable when you do what he wants?"

"It appears that he would have been one too many where I am going. At least that was father

Maurice's opinion, As for me, however, I should have thought that on the contrary it would have been good to see how he would have been received, and that such a pretty child could not have been other than favourably looked upon. But they say at the house that I must not begin by showing the burdens of the family. I don't know why I talk to you about that, little Marie; you know nothing about it."

"Yes I do, Germain, I know that you are going to get married; my mother told me so, desiring me not to speak of it to any one, either at home or where I am going, and you may be easy, I shall not say a word about it."

"You will do well, for it is not yet settled; perhaps I shall not please the woman in question."

"It is to be hoped you will, Germain. Why then should you not please her?"

"Who knows? I have three children, and that is a heavy burden for a woman who is not their mother."

"That is true; but your children are not like other children.'?

"Do you think so?"

"They are beautiful as little angels, and so well brought up that you can't find any more amiable."

"There is Sylvian who is not easy to take care of."

"He is quite small; he cannot be otherwise than terrible; but he has so much spirit!"

"It is true that he has spirit: and a courage! He fears neither cows nor oxen; and if we should let

him, he would climb on the horses' backs with his
eldest brother."

"As for me, in your place, I would have taken
the oldest one. I am very sure it would have made
you loved at once to have such a beautiful child."

"Yes, if the woman loves children: but if she
does not love them?"

"Are there any women who do not love children?"

"Not many, I believe; but there are some, and it
is that which troubles me."

"Then you are not at all acquainted with this
woman?"

"Not more than you; and I fear I shall not be
any better acquainted with her after I have seen her.
I am not suspicious, not I. When any one says fair
words to me, I believe them; but I have more than
once had reason to be sorry for it, for words are not
actions."

"They say that she is a very nice woman."

"Who says so? father Maurice?"

"Yes; your father-in-law."

"That is all very well; but he does not know her
any better."

"Well, you will see her very soon; you must look
quite sharp, and it is to be hoped that you will not
be deceived, Germain."

"Look you, little Marie, I shall be very glad to
have you go to the house a little while before going
straight to Ormeaux; you understand, you have always shown good sense, and you observe every-

thing. If you see anything that makes you think, you will give me notice quite quietly."

"Oh, no! Germain, I shall not do that! I should be too much afraid of being mistaken; and besides, if a word said thoughtlessly should happen to disgust you with this marriage, your relations would blame me; and I have quite troubles enough of my own, without bringing others upon my dear woman of a mother."

As they were talking thus, the Grise pricked up her ears and shied, then retraced her steps and approached the thicket, where something she began to recognise had at first frightened her. Germain cast a glance into the thicket, and saw in the ditch, under the close and still fresh branches of a low oak, something that he took for a lamb.

"There is a beast that has strayed," said he, "or is dead, for it does not move. Perhaps somebody is looking for it; we must see!"

"It is not a beast," cried little Marie; "it's a child asleep: it's your Petit-Pierre!"

"Only think of it!" said Germain, dismounting from the horse; "there is that good-for-nothing fellow asleep there, so far from the house, and in a ditch where some snake might easily find him!"

He took the child in his arms, who smiled upon him as he opened his eyes, and threw his arms round his neck, saying:—

"My little papa, you'll take me with you now!"

"Ah, yes! always the same song! What were you doing there, naughty Pierre?'

"I was waiting for my little papa to pass," said the child; "I kept looking along the road all the time, and I looked so much that I fell asleep."

"And if I had passed without seeing you, you would have remained all night out of doors, and the wolf would have eaten you?"

"Oh! I knew very well that you would see me!" replied Petit-Pierre, confidently.

"Well, now, my Pierre, kiss me, say good-bye, and run back to the house as quick as you can, if you don't want them to eat supper without you."

"Then you won't take me with you?" said the little one, beginning to rub his eyes to show that he intended to cry.

"You know very well that grandfather and grandmother don't wish you to go," said Germain, retrenching himself behind the authority of the old people, like a man who does not depend a great deal on his own.

But the child would listen to nothing. He began to cry in good earnest, saying that since his father was taking little Marie, he could not take him too. He was told that it would be necessary to pass through deep woods, where there were a great many ugly beasts that devoured little children, that the Grise did not wish to carry three persons, she had said so when they started, and that, in the country where they were going, there was neither bed nor supper for little monkeys. All these excellent reasons did not persuade Petit-Pierre, he threw himself down and rolled on the grass, crying that his little papa did not love him any longer, and that if he did not take him he would not go back to the house all night or all day.

Germain had a father's heart, as tender and as weak as that of a woman. The death of his wife, the cares which he had been obliged to bestow alone upon his little ones, as well as the thought that these poor motherless children required a great deal of love, had contributed to make him so, and he had such a hard combat with himself, all the harder because he was ashamed of his weakness, and tried to conceal his discomfort from little Marie, that the sweat stood on his forehead, and his eyes became tinged with red, quite prepared to shed tears likewise. At last he tried to make himself angry, but, on turning towards little Marie as if to call upon her to witness the firmness of his soul, he saw that the face of that good girl was bathed in tears, and all his courage deserting him, it was impossible for him to restrain his, although he scolded and threatened still.

"Really, your heart is too hard," said little Marie to him at last, "and for my part, I should never have strength enough to resist a child who has so great a sorrow. Come, Germain, take him with you. Your mare is quite accustomed to carry two grown persons and a child, since your brother-in-law and his wife, who is a great deal heavier than I am, go to market on Saturdays with their boy, on the back of this good beast. You can put him astride before you, and besides, I would much prefer going on foot rather than give pain to this little one."

"There is no need of that," replied Germain, who was dying with desire to allow himself to be persuaded. "The Grise is strong and could carry two more if there was room on her back. But what shall we do with this child on the road? He will be cold, he will be hungry; and who will take care of him to-night and to-morrow, put him to bed, wash him and dress him again? I shouldn't dare to give that trouble to a woman whom I don't know, and who would think, doubtless, that I used very little ceremony with her at the beginning."

"From the good-will or the dissatisfaction she may show, you will know her at once, believe me, Germain! And besides, if she rejects your Pierre, I will take charge of him. I will go to her house to dress him, and will carry him to the fields to-morrow. I will amuse him the whole day, and be careful that he wants nothing."

"And he will weary you, my poor girl! he will be in your way! a whole day, that's a long while!"

"It will give me pleasure, on the contrary; he will be company for me, and will make me less sad the first day I shall have to pass in a new country. I shall imagine that I am still at home."

The child, seeing that little Marie took his part, had fastened himself to her skirts and held her so strongly that it would have been necessary to hurt him in tearing him from her. When he discovered that his father yielded, he took Marie's hand in his two little hands, orowned by the sun, and kissed her, leaping with joy and dragging her towards the mare with that ardent impatience which children display in their wishes.

"Come! come!" said the young girl, raising him in her arms, "we will try to quiet this poor heart which leaps like a little bird, and if you feel cold when night comes, tell me so, my Pierre, and I will wrap you up in my cape. Kiss your little papa, and ask his pardon for having been naughty. Tell him that it shall never happen again! never, do you understand?"

"Yes, yes, on condition that I always do just as he wants me to, is it not?" said Germain wiping his son's eyes with his handkerchief. "Ah! Marie, you spoil the little scamp for me!—And really, you have too good a heart, little Marie. I don't know why you did not enter as a shepherdess with us at the last Saint John. You would have taken care of my children, and I should have much preferred paying you well for tending them to going after a woman who will perhaps think she does me a favour in not detesting them."

"You must not look at things so much on the bad side," replied little Marie, holding the bridle of the horse while Germain placed his son in front of the large pack-saddle garnished with goat skin; "if your wife does not love the children, you shall take me into your service next year, and you may be easy, I will amuse them so well that they shall perceive nothing of it."

CHAPTER IV.

UNDER THE GREAT OAKS.

'Oh !'' said Germain, after they had ridden a short distance, "what will they say at the house when they don't see this little fellow come back? The parents will be anxious, and will look for him everywhere.''

"You will tell the man who is at work on the road beyond, that you are carrying Pierre with you, and you will ask him to tell your family.''

"That's true, Marie, you think of everything, you do! As for me, I did not even remember that Jeannie must be there.''

"And as he lives quite near the farm, he will not fail to do your message.''

When this precaution had been taken, Germain put the mare to her trot again, and Petit-Pierre was so joyous that he did not immediately perceive he had not dined. But as the motion of the horse hollowed his stomach, he began, after travelling about a league, to yawn, to turn pale and confess that he was dying with hunger.

"There, now he's beginning,'' said Germain. " I

knew that we should not go far before this gentleman would cry that he was hungry or thirsty."

"I'm thirsty too," said Petit-Pierre.

"Very well! Then we will make a stop at moth·r
Rebec's tavern, at Corlay, at the *Break of Day!* A
fine sign, but a poor resting place! Come, Marie,
you also will take a sip of wine."

"No, no, I don't want anything," said she; "I
will hold the mare while you go in with the little
one."

"But now I think of it, my good girl, you gave
your luncheon to my Pierre this morning, and you,
you are fasting; you were not willing to dine with
us at the house, you did nothing but cry."

"Oh, I was not hungry, I was too sorry! and I
swear to you that even now I have no desire to eat."

"You must force yourself, little one; otherwise
you will be sick. We have a long road to travel, and
must not arrive there like famished people who ask
for bread before saying how do you do. I wish to
set you an example myself, though I have no great
appetite; but I shall succeed, inasmuch as I did not
dine either. I saw you crying, you and your mother,
and that troubled my heart. Come, come, I will
fasten the Grise at the door; get down, I wish
you to."

They all three went into Rebec's, and, in less than
a quarter of an hour, the fat lame woman succeeded
in serving them with a good looking omelette, hard
bread, and claret wine.

Peasants do not eat fast; and little Pierre had

such an appetite that it was quite an hour before
Germain could think of starting again. Little Marie
nad eaten from complaisance at first, but by degrees
hunger had come; for at sixteen we cannot diet a
long while, and the air of the country is imperious.
The good words which Germain knew how to say
to her to console her and make her take courage,
also produced their effect; she made an effort to
persuade herself that seven months would soon be
passed, and to think on the happiness she would
nave at finding herself again in her family and village, since father Maurice and Germain agreed together in promising to take her into their service.
But as she began to laugh and sport with little
Pierre, Germain had the unfortunate idea of making
her look, through the tavern window, at the beautiful view of the valley, which can be seen entire
from that height, and which is so smiling, so green,
and so fertile. Marie looked and asked if the houses
of Belair could be seen from there.

"Without doubt," said Germain, "and the farm,
and even your house. There, see, that little grey
point, not far from the great poplar tree at Godard,
just below the clock tower."

"Ah! I see it," said the little one. And thereupon she began to weep.

"I was wrong to make you think of that," said
Germain. "How stupid I am to-day! Come, Marie,
let us go, my girl; the days are short, and in an
nour, when the moon rises, it will not be warm."

They started again, crossed the great *heath*, and as

in order not to tire the young girl and the child 'y
too long a trot, Germain could not make the mare
travel very fast, the sun had set when they left the
road to enter the wood.

Germain knew the road as far as Magnier; but he
thought he would find a shorter one by not taking
the avenue of Chanteloube, and by going through
Presles and Sepulture, a direction which he was not
accustomed to follow when going to the fair. He
was mistaken, and even lost some little time before
entering the wood, and moreover he did not enter it
on the right side, and did not perceive this, so that
he turned his back on Fourche, and went much too
high on the side of Ardennes.

What then prevented him from finding his way
was a fog that rose with the night, one of those
autumn evening mists, which the whiteness of the
moonlight renders still more vague and deceitful.
The great pools of water which are scattered through
the glades exhaled vapours so thick that, when the
Grise passed through them, her riders could not
perceive them, except by the plashing of her feet,
and the difficulty she had in drawing them out of
the mud.

When they had at last found a fine alley quite
straight, and had reached the end, Germain tried to
discover where he was. He found that he was lost;
for father Maurice, in explaining the road to him,
had told him, that on leaving the wood, he would
nave to descend a very steep path, to cross an im-
mense meadow, and pass the river twice by fording.

He had even advised him to be very cautious in passing the river, because there had been heavy rains at the beginning of the season, and the water might be rather high. Seeing neither descent, nor meadow, nor river, but the heath, smooth and white as a sheet of snow, Germain stopped, looked for a house, waited for a passing traveller, and found nothing to direct him. Then he retraced his steps and re-entered the wood. But the fog became still thicker, the moon was completely veiled, the roads were horrible, the quagmires deep. The Grise almost came down twice; loaded as she was, she lost courage, and, if she retained discernment enough not to strike against the trunks of the trees, she could not prevent her riders from having to do with large branches, which barred the road at the height of their heads, and put them in a great deal of danger. Germain lost his hat in one of these encounters, and had much difficulty in finding it again. Petit-Pierre had gone to sleep, and, letting himself hang like a bag, he embarrassed his father's arms so much, that the latter could neither sustain nor guide the horse.

"I believe that we are bewitched," said Germain, stopping; "for these woods are not large enough for a man to lose himself in, unless he were drunk, and here we have been going round and round at least two hours, without being able to get out. The Grise has but one idea in her head, which is to return to the house, and it is she that has made me lose my road. If we want to go home, we have only to let her take her own way. But when we are, perhaps,

fifty two steps from the place where we are to sleep,
we must be really crazy to give up and begin such a
long journey over again. Still, I no longer know
hat to do. I can see neither sky nor ground, and
I fear that the child may catch a fever if we remain
in this cursed fog, or that he may be crushed by our
weight if the mare should give. way in her fore
legs.''

"We must not persist any longer,'' said little
Marie. "Let us get down, Germain ; give me the
child, I can carry him very well, and will prevent
the cape from leaving him uncovered, when it blows
aside better than you can. You will lead the mare
by the bridle, and perhaps we shall see more clearly
when we are nearer the ground.''

This method succeeded only in saving them from
a fall of the horse, for the fog crept along and seemed
to glue itself to the moist earth. They walked with
difficulty, and were soon so harrassed that they stopped, on at last finding a dry place under the great
oaks. Little Marie was completely wet, but she did
not complain, and was in no degree anxious about
herself. Busied solely with the child, she seated
herself upon the sand, and laid him on her lap, while
Germain explored the environs, after having fastened
the Grise's bridle to the branch of a tree.

But the Grise, who was very much tired of this
journey, made a sudden plunge, unfastened the bridle, broke her girths, and, flinging up her heels
higher than her head, by way of farewell, half a
dozen times darted off through the thicket, showing

very clearly that she had no need of any one to help
her to find the road.

"There," said Germain, after having tried in vain
to catch her, "now we are unhorsed, and it would
do us no good to find the true path, for we should
have to pass the river on foot; and to see how these
roads are full of water, we may be very sure that the
meadow is under the river. We do not know the
other passages. We must wait till the fog goes off;
it cannot last more than an hour or two. When we
can see clearly we will look for a house, the first we
can find on the border of the wood; but now we
cannot get away from here; there is a ditch, a
swamp, I don't know what, right in front of us; and
behind I don't know any better what there is, for I
can no longer tell by which side we came."

"Well! let us take patience, Germain," said
little Marie. "We are quite well enough on this
small height. The rain does not come through the
leaves of these great oaks, and we can light a fire,
for I feel some old roots, which are not fastened to
anything, and which are dry enough to blaze. You
have a light, haven't you, Germain? You were
smoking your pipe just now."

"I had one! my tinder-box was on the pack-saddle, in my bag, with the game I was carrying to my
intended; but that cursed mare has run off with
everything, even my cloak, which she will lose, and
tear against all the branches "

"Not so, Germain; the pack-saddle, the cloak,
the nag, everything is there, on the ground, close by

your feet. The Grise broke her girths, and threw
them all off, when she ran away."

"*Vrai Dieu*, so it is!" said the husbandman,
"and if we can find a little dead wood by feeling
about, we shall make out to dry ourselves and get
warm."

"There is no difficulty about that," said little
Marie, "the dead wood crackles everywhere as you
step; but hand me the pack-saddle here first of
all."

"What do you want to do with it?"

"To make a bed for the little one. No, not so!—
upside down; he will not roll out of the hollow;
and it is still quite warm from the back of the beast.
Prop it up on both sides with those stones you see
there."

"I cannot see them, not I! You must have the
eyes of a cat!"

"There, now it's done, Germain! Give me your
cloak, so that I may wrap up his little feet, and I'll
put my cape over his body. See! if he is not lying
there as comfortable as in his bed! and feel how
warm he is!"

"That's true! you know how to take care of children, Marie!"

"There's not much magic in that. Now look in
your bag for your tinder-box, and I will put the
wood together."

"This wood will never catch, it's too damp."

"You doubt everything, Germain! don't you recollect then having been a *pastour*, and having made

great fires in the fields, in the very midst of the rain."

"Yes, that's the talent of the children who tend flocks ; but as for me, I was a driver of oxen as soon as I could walk."

"That's the reason why you are stronger in your arms than skilful with your hands. There now, the wood is ready, you shall see if it will not blaze ! give me the fire and a handful of dry grass. That's right ! now blow, you are not consumptive ?"

"Not that I know of," said Germain, blowing like a blacksmith's bellows.

A moment after, the flame burst out, cast a red light at first, and ended by rising in bluish jets under the foliage of the oaks, struggling against the mist, and drying the atmosphere by degrees for ten feet round.

"Now I will take my seat by the side of the little one, so that no sparks shall fall on him," said the young girl. "Do you put on some wood and keep up the fire, Germain! We shall get neither fever nor cold here, I'll warrant you."

"Faith, you're a girl of sense," said Germain, "and you know how to make a fire like a witch of the night. I feel myself quite restored, and my heart comes back to me ; for with my legs wet up to my knees, and the idea of remaining so till daylight, I was in a very bad humour just now."

"And when you're in a bad humour, you can think of nothing," returned little Marie.

"You are never in a bad humour then, are you ?"

F

" Oh no ! never.   What good would it do ?"

" Oh ! it does no good, certainly ; but how can
you help it, when you have troubles ? God knows
that you have had enough of them, nevertheless,
my poor little one, for you haven't always been
happy."

That's true, we have suffered, my poor mother
and I.   We have had sorrows, but we have never
lost courage."

" I should never lose my courage for any work
whatever," said Germain ; " but poverty would vex
me ; for I have never been in want of anything.   My
wife made me rich, and I am so still ; I shall be so
as long as I work at the farm.   That will be always,
I hope—but every one must have his troubles, I have
suffered in other ways."

" Yes, you have lost your wife, and that's a great
pity !"

" Isn't it ?"

" Oh ! I cried a great deal for her, you may be
sure, Germain ! for she was so good !   Come don't
let us talk about her ; I should cry for her again ; all
my troubles seem to be coming back to-day "

" It is true that she loved you a great deal, little
Marie ! she thought very well of you and your
mother.   Come, now you are crying ? Look you,
my girl, I don't want to cry, I—"

" And yet you cry, nevertheless, Germain ! You
cry, also ! Why should a man be ashamed to cry
for his wife ? Don't restrain yourself, don't !
really go shares with you in that sorrow !"

"You have a good heart, Marie, and it does me good to cry with you. But put your feet close to the fire; your skirts are all wet too, poor girl! Come, I will take your place by the little one, warm yourself better than that.'

"I am warm enough," said Marie, "and if you want to sit down, take a corner of the cloak, I am well enough."

"The fact is that we are not badly off here," said Germain taking a seat close beside her. "There is nothing but hunger that troubles me a little. It must be quite nine o'clock in the evening, and I had so much difficulty in walking in these bad roads, that I feel quite weakened. Are you not hungry, you too, Marie?"

"I? not at all. I am not used to make four meals like you. And I have gone to bed so many times without supper, that once more does not make much difference to me."

"Well! a wife like you is quite convenient; she does not spend much," said Germain smiling.

"I am not a wife," said Marie naively, without perceiving the turn which the finished ploughman's ideas were taking. "Are you dreaming?"

"Yes, I believe I am dreaming," said Germain; "perhaps it is hunger makes me wander!"

"What a glutton you are then!" returned she, a little sportive in her turn; well! if you can't live five or six hours without eating, haven't you game there in your bag and fire to cook it with

"Diantre! that's a good idea! but the present to my future father-in-law?"

"You have six partridges and a hare! I think you don't require all that to satisfy your hunger?"

"But how to cook anything here, without spit or andirons? It would be burnt to a coal.

"Not so," said little Marie, "I will undertake to cook it for you under the ashes without a taste of smoke. Have you never caught larks in the fields, and have you never cooked them between two stones? Ah! it is true! I forgot you have never been a *pastour*. Come, pick this partridge! not so hard! you pull off the skin!"

"You might very well pick the other to show me!"

"Then you mean to eat two of them? What an ogre! there, now they are picked, I will cook them."

"You would make a perfect sutler, little Marie; but as bad luck would have it, you have no canteen, and I shall be compelled to drink the water of this pool."

"You would like some wine isn't it so? Perhaps you must have your coffee? You think yourself at the fair under the arbour! Call the innkeeper: some liquor for the finished ploughman of Belair!"

"Ah, you naughty little girl, you are laughing at me? You wouldn't drink any wine if you had it, you know you wouldn't?"

"I! I drank some with you this evening, at the Rebec's, for the second time in my life; if you are very good, I will give you a bottle almost full, and of good wine too!"

" How, Marie, you are a witch then decidedly ? "

" Weren't you so foolish as to ask for two bottles of wine at the Rebec's ? You drank one with your boy, and I hardly swallowed three drops of that which you placed before me. Still you paid for them both, without looking at it."

" Well ? "

" Well ! I put in my basket that which had not been drunk, because I thought that you or your little one might be thirsty on the road, and here it is."

" You are the most wide-awake girl I ever met with. What! She was crying, nevertheless, poor child, when she left the inn ! That did not prevent her from thinking of others more than of herself. Little Marie, the man that marries you will not be a fool ! "

" I hope so, for I could not love a fool. Come, eat your partridges, they are cooked to a turn ; and, for want of bread, you must be satisfied with chestnuts."

" And where the devil have you got chestnuts from too ? "

" That is very astonishing ! all along the road, I took them from the branches as we passed, and I filled my pockets."

" And they are cooked too ? "

" What should I have been thinking of, if I had not put them into the fire as soon as it was lighted ? We always do so in the fields,"

" Ah then. little Marie, we will sup together ! I wish to drink to your health, and wish you a good

husband—there, such as you would wish yourself.
Tell me a little about him.'

"I should find that hard, Germain, for I have not
yet thought of one."

"How? not at all? never?" said Germain, beginning to eat with a ploughman's appetite, but cutting
off the best pieces to offer to his companion, who
refused obstinately, and contented herself with a few
chestnuts. "Tell me then, little Marie," resumed
he. seeing that she did not think of answering him,
"have you not had any idea of marrying? You are
old enough, nevertheless."

"Perhaps so," said she; "but I am too poor. I
must have at least a hundred crowns to go to house-
keeping with, and I must work five or six years at
least to get them."

"Poor girl! I wish father Maurice would give me
a hundred crowns to make you a present of."

"Many thanks, Germain! Well! What would
they say of me?"

"What should you expect them to say? They
know very well that I am old, and that I cannot
marry you. Then they would not suppose that I—
that you—"

"Come, come, husbandman! there's your boy
waking up," said little Marie.

CHAPTER V.

IN SPITE OF THE COLD.

LITTLE Pierre had risen, and was looking round him with quite a pensive air.

"Ah! he never does anything else when he hears any eating going on, not he!" said Germain. "You might fire a cannon in his ear and not wake him; but if you move your jaws near him, he opens his eyes at once."

"You must have been just so at his age," said little Marie with a sly smile. "Come, my little Pierre, are you looking for your bed-tester? It is made of leaves, to-night, my child; but your father is taking his supper, nevertheless. Do you want to sup with him? I have not eaten your share; I was pretty sure you would claim it."

"Marie, I wish you to eat," cried the husbandman, "I will not eat any more. I am a voracious glutton; you deprive yourself of everything for us, that is not right, and I feel ashamed of myself. Look you, it takes away my hunger; I don't wish my son to have any supper, unless you eat some."

"Let us alone," said little Marie, "you have not the key of our appetites. Mine is shut up to-day, while your Pierre's is open like that of a little wolf. Look, see how he takes hold! oh! he also will be a hard workman."

In fact, Petit-Pierre soon showed whose son he was, and barely awake, understanding neither where he was nor how he came there, he began to devour. Then, when he no longer felt hungry, finding himself excited, as happens to children when their regular habits are broken, he had more sense, more curiosity, and more reasoning powers than usual. He made them explain to him where he was, and when he learnt that he was in the middle of a wood he was a little frightened.

"Are there any ugly beasts in this wood?" asked he of his father.

"No," said the father, "there are none. You needn't be afraid."

"Then you told me a story when you said that if I went with you into the woods the wolves would carry me off?"

"See what a reasoner he is," said Germain, embarrassed.

"He is right." returned little Marie, "you did tell him so; he has a good memory, he recollects it. But you must know, my Petit-Pierre, that your father never tells a story. We passed through the great woods while you were asleep, and now we are in the little woods, where there are no ugly beasts."

"Are the little woods very far from the great ones?'

"Quite far; besides, the wolves never go out of the great woods. And then if any should come here, your father would kill them."

"And you too, little Marie?"

"And we too; for you would help us a great deal, my Pierre. You are not afraid, are you? You would hit them a good hard knock!"

"Yes, yes," said the child, emboldened, and taking a heroic posture; "we would kill them!"

"There is nobody like you to talk to little children," said Germain to little Marie, "and to make them hear reason. It is true that it is not long since you were a child yourself, and you remember what your mother used to say to you. I really believe that the younger we are, the better understanding we can have with those that are so. I am very much afra'd that a woman of thirty, who does not yet know what it is to be a mother, will find some difficulty in learning how to chat and to reason with my little ones."

"Why so, then, Germain? I don't know why you have a bad idea about that woman; you will get over it!"

"The devil take the woman!" said Germain. "I wish I was back at home never to return. What do I want with a wife I don't know?"

"My little papa," said the child, "what is the reason that you are always talking of your wife to-day? Since she is dead?——"

"Alas! then you have not forgotten her, your poor dear mother?"

"No, since I saw her put into a beautiful box of white wood, and grandmother took me afterwards to kiss her and bid her good-bye! She was quite white and cold; and every night my aunt makes me pray to the good God that she may go and warm herself with him in heaven. Do you believe she is there now?"

"I hope so, my child; but you must always pray, that makes your mother see that you love her."

"I will say my prayer now," said the child; "I did not think to say it this evening. But I can't say it all alone; I always forget some of it. Little Marie must help me."

"Yes, my Pierre, I will help you," said the young girl. "Come here, kneel on me."

The child knelt down on the young girl's skirt, clasped his little hands, and began to recite his prayer—at first with attention and fervour, for he knew the beginning very well; then with more slowness and hesitation; and at last repeating word by word what little Marie dictated to him, when he reached that part of his petition where, sleep overpowering him every evening, he had never been able to learn to the end. This time, also, the labour of attention and the monotony of his own accent produced their accustomed effect; he no longer pronounced the last syllables without effort, and even after having them repeated to him three times; his head became heavy and bowed itself upon Marie's bosom; his hands opened, separated, and fell stretched out upon his knees. By the light of the bivouac fire, Germain looked at his little angel asleep on the heart of the young girl, who, supporting him in her arms, and warming his blond tresses with her pure breath, had also allowed herself to sink into a pious reverie, and was praying mentally for Catherine's soul.

Germain was affected, sought for something to say to little Marie, in order to express to her his esteem and gratitude, but could find nothing that would explain his thought. He approached her to kiss his son, whom she still held pressed to her bosom, and he found some difficulty in taking his lips away from Petit-Pierre's forehead.

"You kiss him too hard," said Marie, gently pushing away the husbandman's head; "you will wake him up. Let me put him to bed again, since he has fallen back into his dreams of Paradise."

The child allowed himself to be laid down; but on stretching himself upon the goat-skin of the pack-saddle, he asked if he was on the Grise's back. Then, opening his great blue eyes, and keeping them fixed towards the branches for a minute, he seemed to be dreaming wide awake, or to be struck by some idea which had glided into his mind during the day, and which there took form at the approach of sleep.

"My little papa," said he, "if you wish to give me another mamma, I want it to be little Marie."

And, without waiting for an answer, he closed his eyes and fell sound asleep.

Little Marie appeared to pay no other attention to the strange words of the child than to look upon them as a proof of friendship; she wrapped him up with care, renewed the fire, and, as the fog sleeping upon the neighbouring pool did not appear in any manner about to lighten, she advised Germain to lie down by the fire and take a nap.

'I see that you are getting sleepy," said she to him, "for you don't say a word now, and you are looking at the coals just as your little one did a short time ago. Come, go to sleep; I will take care of the child and the fire."

" It is you who will go to sleep," replied the husbandman, "and I will guard you both, for I never had less desire to sleep; I have fifty ideas in my head."

"Fifty! that's a great many," said the young girl, with rather a mocking accent; "there are so many people who would be lucky to have a single one!"

"Well, if I am not capable of having fifty, I have at least one that has not left me for more than an hour."

"And I will tell you what it is, as well as that which you had before."

"Well, yes! tell it if you guess it, Marie; tell it to me yourself, it will give me pleasure."

"An hour ago," returned she, "you had the idea of eating, and now you have the idea of sleeping."

"Marie, I am only an ox-driver, but really you take me for an ox. You are a naughty girl, and I see very well that you do not wish to talk to me. Go to sleep, then ; that would be better than to criticise a man who is not gay."

" If you want to talk, let us talk," said the little girl, half lying down by the child's side, and resting her head upon the pack-saddle. " You are inclined to torment yourself, Germain ; and in that you do not show much courage for a man.. What should not I say myself, if I did not strive the best in my power against my own troubles?"

" Yes, without doubt ; and it is exactly that I am thinking about, my poor child ! You are going to live far away from your relations, and in an ugly country of heaths and swamps, where you will get the autumn fevers. and where woolly animals do not thrive. which always vexes a shepherdess of good intentions ; and then you will be among strangers who, perhaps, will not be good to you—who will not understand your value. There, it gives me more pain and sorrow than I can tell you ; and I have a great mind to carry you back to your mother instead of going to Fourche."

" You talk with a great deal of goodness, but without reason, my poor Germain ; we ought not to be cowardly for our friends, and, instead of showing me the bad side of my lot, you ought to show me the good one, as you did when we were eating at the Rebecs."

" What would you have me do ? It appeared so to me at that time, and now it appears otherwise ; you would do better to find a husband."

"That cannot be, Germain, I have told you; and as it cannot be, I do not think of it."

"But in fine if one could be found? Perhaps if you would tell me what sort of a man you would wish him to be, I should succeed in imagining some one."

"Imagining is not finding. As for me, I imagine nothing, because it is useless "

"You would not have an idea of finding a rich one?"

"No, certainly not, because I'm as poor as Job.

"But if he was in comfortable circumstances, it wouldn't trouble you to have a good house, good food, good clothes, and to be in a family of honest people, who would permit you to help your mother?'

"Oh! as to that, yes. To help my mother is all I desire."

"And if that could be found, even when the man was not in his first youth, you would not be too difficult?"

"Ah! excuse me, Germain. That is exactly what I should lay stress upon. I could not love an old man."

"An old man, no doubt; but a man of my age for instance."

"Your age is old for me, Germain; I should rather prefer the age of Bastien, though Bastien is not so handsome a man as you."

"You would prefer Bastien, the swine-herd?" said Germain, with some ill-humour. "A boy that has eyes made like the beast he drives?"

"I should pass over his eyes, on account of his eighteen years."

Germain felt horribly jealous.

"Come," said he, "I see that you have some feeling for Bastien. That's an odd idea, none the less."

"Yes, that would be an odd idea," replied little Marie, "and he would make an odd sort of husband. You can make him believe everything you choose. For instance, the other day, I had picked up a tomato, in M. the curate's garden; I told him it was a fine red apple, and he bit into it like a glutton. If you had only seen the face he made! *Mon Dieu*, now ugly he was!"

"Then you don't love him, since you laugh at him?"

"That would be no reason. But I do not love him; he treats his sister like a brute, and he is dirty."

"Well, don't you feel a liking for somebody else?"

"What is that to you, Germain?"

"Oh! nothing, it is only to talk. I see very well, little girl, that you have a gallant already in your head."

"No, Germain, you are mistaken, I have none as yet; that may come by and by: but since I shall not marry until I have saved something, I am destined to be married late and to an old man."

"Well, take an old man now, at once."

"Not so; when I am no longer young myself, that will be all the same to me; now, it would be different."

"I see very well, Marie, that I do not please you, that is clear enough," said Germain with vexation, and without weighing his words.

Little Marie did not answer. Germain leaned towards her—she had fallen overpowered, and as if stricken down by slumber, as do children who fall asleep even while they are still chatting.

Germain was glad that she had paid no attention to his last words; he acknowledged to himself that they were not wise; and he turned his back upon her, in order that he might distract and change his thoughts.

But, do his best, he could neither sleep nor think of anything else than what he had just said. He turned twenty times round the fire, he went to a distance, he came back again; at last, feeling as agitated as if he had swallowed gunpowder, he rested against the tree that sheltered the two children, and looked at them asleep.

"I don't know why I never perceived," thought he, "that this little Marie is the prettiest girl of the country. She has not much colour, but she has a little face as fresh as a wild rose. What a pretty mouth and what a darling little nose! She is not large for her age; but she is made like a young quail, and is as light as a lark. I don't know why they think so much with us about great fat red women. My wife was rather small and pale, and she pleased me above all. This one is quite delicate, but she has none the more ill health for that; and she is pretty to look at as a white kid. And then what a sweet and honest air! How you can read her good heart in her eyes, even when they are closed in sleep! As to sense, she has more of that than my good Catherine had; and a man would never feel wearied with her. She is gay; she is steady; she is industrious; she is loving; and she is droll!—I don't see what a man can wish for better!

"But why am I thinking about all this?" resumed Germain, trying to look another way; "my father-in-law would never listen to it; and the whole family would treat me as a crazy man. Besides, she herself would not wish to take me, the poor child She thinks I am too old, she has told me so; she is not self-interested; she cares but little for having poverty and trouble, for wearing poor clothes and suffering with hunger two or three months in the year, provided she can satisfy her heart some day, and give herself to a husband who will please her. She is right; that she is! I would do the same in her place; and, from this moment, if I could follow my own will, and instead of embarking in a marriage that has no pleasant aspect for me, I would choose a girl to my liking."

The more Germain tried to reason with and to calm himself, the less he succeeded. He went off twenty paces from the spot, to lose himself in the fog, and suddenly found himself on his knees by the side of the two sleeping children. Once even, he wished to kiss his little Pierre, who had an arm round Marie's neck, and he deceived himself so much

that Marie, feeling a breath hot as fire pass over her
lips, woke up and looked at him with a frightened
air, understanding nothing of all that was taking
place in him.

"I did not see you, my poor children," said Germain, retiring very quickly. "I came near falling
on you and hurting you."

Little Marie had the candour to believe him, and
went to sleep again. Germain passed to the other
side of the fire, and swore to God that he would not
stir from there until she woke up. He kept his oath,
but not without difficulty. He thought he should
become crazy.

At last, towards midnight, the fog cleared off, and
Germain could see the stars shine through the trees.
The moon also freed herself from the vapours which
covered her, and began to sprinkle diamonds over
the wet moss. The trunks of the oaks remained in
a majestic obscurity; but a little further off, the
white stems of the birches looked like a rank of
phantoms in their winding-sheets. The fire was reflected in the pool, and the frogs, becoming accustomed to it, ventured some shrill and timid notes.
The angular branches of the old trees, gristly with
pale lichens, stretched out and crossed each other
like great fleshless arms over the heads of our travellers. It was a beautiful spot, but so desert and so
sad, that Germain, tired of suffering there, began to
sing and to throw stones into the pool in order to
relieve his mind from the frightful ennui of the solitude. He also wished to wake little Marie; and

when he saw that she rose and looked at the weather, ne proposed to her to set off again.

"In two hours," said he to her, "the approach of day will make it so cold that we shall not be able to bear it, in spite of our fire. Now, we can see our way, and we shall easily find a house that will open to us, or at least some barn in which we can pass the rest of the night under cover."

Marie had no will of her own, and though she still felt a strong inclination to sleep, she got ready to follow Germain. The latter took his son in his arms without waking him, and wished that Marie should come near to him so as to be covered by his cloak, as she was not willing to take back her cape, which was rolled round little Pierre.

When he felt the young girl so near to him, Germain, who had been cheered and enlivened for a moment, again began to lose his wits. Two or three times he moved suddenly away from her, and left her to walk alone; then, seeing that she had some difficulty in following him, he waited for her, drew her quickly towards him, and pressed her so strongly, that she was astonished and even vexed at it without daring to complain.

As they knew nothing of the direction in which they started, so they knew no better that which they followed. So much was this the case, that they traversed the whole wood once more, found themselves again in front of the desert heath, retraced their steps, and after having turned and walked a long while, at last perceived a light through the branches.

"Good, here's a house!" said Germain, " and people already up, since the fire is lighted. It must be very late, then?"

But there was no house; it was their bivouac fire, which they had covered up when they went away, and which the breeze had lighted again. They had walked for two hours only to find themselves again at their point of departure.

CHAPTER VI.

THE LIONESS OF THE VILLAGE.

"This time I give up," said Germain, stamping on the ground. "There's a spell on us, that is very sure; and we shall not get away from here except in broad daylight. This place must be bewitched."

"Come, come, don't let us be vexed," said Marie, "and let us do the best we can. We will make up a large fire; the child is so well wrapped up that there is no risk for him; and it won't kill us to pass a night out of doors. Where have you hidden the pack-saddle, Germain? In the middle of that holly, crazy fellow? It's very convenient to get at it again!"

"Here, take the child, while I pull his bed out of the thorns; I don't want you to wound your hands."

"It is done—here is the bed, and a few pricks are not sword cuts," said the brave little girl.

She proceeded anew to put to bed Petit-Pierre, who was so sound asleep this time that he had known nothing of their last journey. Germain put so much wood on the fire that the whole forest shone around

them; but little Marie could do no more, and though
she did not complain, she could hardly support herself on her feet.   She was pale, and her teeth chattered with cold and weakness.   Germain took her in
his arms to warm her; and anxiety, compassion, feelings of irresistible tenderness, taking possession of his
heart, silenced his senses.   His tongue was loosed
by a miracle, and all shame ceasing—

"Marie!" said he to her, "you please me, and I
am very unhappy because I do not please you.   If
you would accept me for your husband, there would
be neither father-in-law, nor relations, nor neighbours, nor advice, that should prevent my giving
myself to you.   I know that you would make my
children happy; that you would teach them to respect the memory of their mother; and, my conscience being at peace, I could satisfy my heart.   I
have always felt a friendship for you; and now I feel
so much in love, that, if you should ask me to do
your thousand wishes all my life, I would swear it
to you this moment.   See, I beseech you, how much
I love you, and try to forget my age.   Think that it
is a false notion you form when you believe that a
man of thirty is old.   Besides, I am only twenty-
eight.   A young girl fears that she will be criticised
if she takes a man who is ten or twelve years older
than herself, because it is not the custom of the
country; but I have been told that in other coun-
tries they do not look at that; that, on the contrary,
they prefer to give, as a support to a young person,
a man who is reasonable and of tried courage, rather

than a young lad who may change, and from a good
fellow, as he was thought to be, turn into a good-for-
nothing scamp. Besides, years do not always make
the age. That depends on the health and strength
one has. When a man is worn out by too much
labour and poverty, or bad conduct, he is old before
he reaches twenty-five. Instead of which, I—but
you do not listen to me, Marie."

"Yes I do, Germain. I hear you very well," replied little Marie; "but I am thinking of what my
mother has often told me: which is that a woman
of sixty is much to be pitied when her husband is
seventy or seventy-five years old, and can no longer
work for her support. He becomes infirm, and she
must nurse him at an age when she herself would
begin to have great need of nursing and repose. It
is thus they come to end upon the straw."

"The parents are right in saying that, I allow,
Marie," returned Germain; but they would sacrifice
the whole time of youth, which is the best, to guard
against what will happen at the age when one is no
longer good for anything, and when it is perfectly
indifferent to end in one manner or another. But
as for me, I am not in danger of dying with hunger
in my old days. I am in a situation to save up
something, because, living with my wife's relations,
I work a great deal and spend nothing. Besides, I
shall love you so much, do you see, that that will
prevent my growing old. They say that when a
man is happy, it preserves him, and I do feel indeed
that I am younger than Bastien to love you; for he

does not love you, not he, he is too much of an animal, too much of a child to understand how pretty
and good you are, and made to be admired. Come,
Marie, do not detest me, I am not a wicked man: I
made my Catherine happy, she said before God on
her death-bed that she had never had anything but
content with me, and she advised me to marry again.
It seems that her spirit spoke this evening to her
child, at the moment when he was falling asleep.
Did you not hear what he said? and how his little
mouth trembled, while his eyes looked at something
in the air which we could not see! He saw his
mother, you may be sure of that, and it was she who
made him say that he wished you to replace her."

"Germain," replied Marie, quite astonished and
pensive, " you speak honestly, and what you say is
true. I am sure I should do well to love you, if it
did not dissatisfy your relations too much : but what
can you wish me to do? my heart does not speak to
me for you. I love you very well, but though your
age does not make you ugly, it frightens me. It
seems to me that you are something like an uncle or
a god-father to me, that I owe you respect, and that
there would be times when you would treat me as a
little girl rather than as your wife and equal. And
besides, my comrades would perhaps laugh at me,
and though it is foolish to care anything for that,
I believe that I should feel ashamed and a little sad
on my wedding day."

"Those are childish reasons; you talk entirely
like a child, Marie!"

"Well! yes, I am a child," said she, "and it is on that very account I fear too reasonable a man. You see very well that I am too young for you, if you are not too old for me, since already you reproach me for speaking without reason! I cannot have more reason than belongs to my age."

"Alas! *Mon Dieu*, how much I am to be pitied for being so awkward, and for saying so badly what I think!" cried Germain. "Marie, you do not love me, that is the fact; you consider me too simple and too heavy. If you did love me, you would not see my faults so clearly. But you do not love me, that is it."

"Well, it's not my fault," returned she, a little wounded by what he had said; "I do the best I can in listening to you: but the more I try the less I can persuade myself that we ought to be husband and wife."

Germain did not answer. He bowed his head upon his hands, and it was impossible for little Marie to know if he wept, if he was vexed, or if he slept. She was a little anxious at seeing him so gloomy, and at not knowing what he was revolving in his mind; but she did not dare to speak to him again; and as she was too much astonished at what had taken place to have any inclination to sleep, she waited for daylight with impatience, always tending the fire and watching over the child, whom Germain appeared no longer to remember. Still Germain did not sleep; he did not reflect upon his fate; and formed neither projects of courage nor plans of seduction. He suffered, he had a mountain of sorrows on his heart. He could have wished he were dead. It appeared that everything must turn out badly for him, and if he could have shed tears, he would not have done it by halves. But he felt a little anger against himself, mingled with his pain, and he was smothering without being able or willing to complain.

When daylight came, and the noises of the country announced it to Germain, he lifted his face from his hands and rose. He saw that little Marie had not slept any more than he, but he knew not what to say to testify his anxiety. He was completely discouraged. He hid the Grise's pack-saddle again in the bushes, took his bag on his shoulder, and, holding his little one by the hand:

"Now, Marie," said he, "we will try to finish our journey. Do you wish me to go with you to Ormeaux?"

"We will leave the wood together," replied she, "and when we know where we are, we will each go our way."

Germain did not reply. He was hurt that the young girl did not ask him to go with her to Ormeaux, and he did not perceive that he had offered to do so in a tone which seemed to provoke a refusal.

A wood-cutter, whom they met about two hundred paces off, put them in a good path, and told them, that after having passed the great meadow, they had only to go, one quite straight and the other little to the left, in order to reach their respective

stopping places, which were moreover so near each
otl er, that you could plainly see the houses of
Fourche from the farm of Ormeaux and reciprocally.

When they had thanked and passed the wood-
cutter, he called them back, to ask if they had not
lost a horse.

"I found," said he to them, "a handsome grey
mare in my yard, where, perhaps, the wolf compelled her to seek a refuge. My dogs spent the night
in barking, and at daybreak I found the beast under
my shed; she is there now. Go there, and if you
recognise her, take her with you,"

Germain, having given beforehand a description
of the Grise, and being satisfied that it was indeed
she, started off to get his pack-saddle. Then little
Marie offered to carry his child with her to Ormeaux,
where he would come to get him, after he had made
his entrance into Fourche.

"He is not so neat as he should be, after the night
we have passed," said she. "I will clean his clothes;
I will wash his pretty face; I will comb him; and
when he is handsome and tidy, you can present h
to your new family."

"And who tells you that I shall go to Fourche
replied Germain, with some ill humour. "Perh
I shall not go there."

"Oh yes, Germain, you ought to go there; yo
will go there!" returned she.

"You are in a great hurry to have me married to
another, so that you may be sure I shall not plague
you any more."

"Come, Germain, don't think any more of that; it was an idea that came to you in the night, because this unfortunate adventure had somewhat disturbed your mind. But now your reason must come back to you; I promise you that I will forget what you said, and never speak of it to any one."

"Oh! speak of it if you choose. I am not accustomed to take back my words. What I said to you was true, honest—and I shouldn't blush for it before anybody."

"Yes, but if your intended knew, that at the moment of visiting her you had thought of another, that would disincline her towards you. So, you must pay attention to what you say now; don't look at me in that way before people, with such a singular manner. Think of father Maurice, who depends on your obedience, and who would be quite angry with me if I should deter you from doing what he wishes. Good-bye, Germain, I take Petit-Pierre with me, in order to compel you to go to Fourche. He is a pledge I keep for you."

"Then you wish to go with her?" said the husbandman to his son, seeing that he fastened himself to little Marie's hands, and that he followed her resolutely.

"Yes, papa," said the child, who had heard and comprehended after his manner what had been said, without distrust, before him. "I am going with my darling Marie; you will come and get me when you have done being married: but I want Marie to be my little mother."

"You see very well that he wishes it, as well as I," said Germain to the little girl. "Listen, Petit-Pierre," added he, "I want her to be your mother, and to stay always with you. It is she who does not wish to. Try and make her grant to you what she refuses to me."

"You may be easy, papa, I will make her say yes; little Marie always does what I want her to."

He departed with the young girl. Germain remained alone, more sad, more irresolute than ever.

Still, when he had repaired the disorder of the journey, in his clothes, and in the furniture of his horse, when he was mounted on the Grise, and had had the road to Fourche shown to him, he thought that he could no longer draw back, and that he must forget that night of agitation as a dangerous dream.

He found father Leonard on the threshold of his white house, seated on a handsome wooden bench, painted green-spinage colour. There were six stone steps arranged in a flight, which showed that the house had a cellar. The wall of the garden, and the hemp-close, was plastered with lime and sand. It was a beautiful habitation. You would almost have taken it for a citizen's house.

The future father-in-law advanced towards Germain, and after having asked him, for five minutes, the news of his whole family, he added the phrase consecrated by custom, to question politely those whom one meets respecting the object of their journey.

"*So you have come to take a stroll this way?*"

"I have come to see you," replied the husband-

man, "and to make you this little' present of game
from my father-in-law, telling you, also, from him,
that you must know with what intentions I come to
your house."

"Ah, ah!" said father Leonard, laughing, and
slapping his well rounded stomach, "I see, I understand, I have it!"

And, winking his eye, he added:

"You will not be the only one to make your com-
pliments, my young man. There are already three
in the house who are waiting like you. As for myself, I send no one away. I should be very undecided about giving a preference to either, for they
are all good matches. Nevertheless, on account of
father Maurice, and the quality of the soil you cul-
tivate, I should rather like it would be you. But
my daughter is of age, and mistress of her property;
she will therefore act according to her own notions.
Enter, make yourself known; I hope you may get
the good number."

"Pardon, excuse me," replied Germain, quite
surprised to find himself a supernumerary where he
had expected to be alone. "I did not know that
your daughter was already provided with suitors,
and I did not come to contend with others."

"If you thought, because you delayed coming,"
replied father Leonard, without losing his good humour, "that my daughter was still unprovided, you
were greatly mistaken, my boy. Catherine has
wherewithal to attract marrying men, and she will
have only the puzzle of choosing. But enter the house,

I tell you, and do not lose courage. She is a woman
that is well worth the trouble of contending for."

And pushing Germain by the shoulders with a
rough gaiety:

"Come, Catherine," cried he, as he entered the
house, "here is another!"

This jovial but coarse manner of being presented
to the widow, in the presence of her other suitors,
completed the vexation and dissatisfaction of the
husbandman, He felt awkward, and remained for
some moments without daring to raise his eyes upon
the beauty and her court.

Widow Guerin was quite well made and did not
want freshness. But she had an expression in her
face and toilette which displeased Germain at the
very first glance. She had a bold air and appeared
well satisfied with herself; and her cap, garnished
with a triple row of lace, her silk apron and her
neckerchief of black blond, hardly corresponded with
the idea he had formed to himself of a serious and
well-conducted widow. That pretension of dress,
and those free manners, made him think her both
old and ugly, though she was neither one nor the
other. He thought that such a pretty dress and
such cheerful manners would be suitable to the age
and sprightly mind of little Marie, but that this
widow had a heavy and venturesome wit, and that
she wore her fine ornaments without becoming them.

The three suitors were seated at a table loaded
with wines and meats, which was always there ready
for them every Sunday morning; for father Leonard

liked to show his wealth, and the widow was not un-
willing to display her handsome plate and to sit at
the head of the table like a gentlewoman. Germain,
simple and confiding as he was, observed these
things with a good deal of penetration; and, for the
first time in his life, kept on the defensive, while he
touched glasses. Father Leonard had compelled
him to take a place with his rivals, and seating
himself in front of him, he treated him in the best
manner he could, and attended to him with preference. The present of game, in spite of the breach
Germain had made in it on his own account, was
still copious enough to produce its effect. The
widow appeared sensible to it, and the suitors cast
upon it glances of disdain. Germain felt uncomfortable in this company, and did not eat with a good
appetite. Father Leonard rallied him about it.

"You are very sad," said he to him, "and you
make wry faces at your glass. Love must not take
away your appetite; for a gallant who is fasting cannot find pretty words like one who has cleared his
ideas with a little drop of wine."

Germain was mortified to have it supposed that
he was already in love, and the affected air of the
widow, who cast down her eyes smilingly, like a
person sure of her power, gave him a desire to pro-
test against his pretended defeat; but he feared to
seem uncivil, smiled, and took patience. The
widow's gallants appeared to him three rustics.
They must needs be very rich for her to admit their
pretensions. One was more than forty, and almost

as fat as father Leonard; the other was blind of an
eye, and drank enough to stultify himself. The
third was young and quite a pretty boy; but he
wished to pass for a wit and said such flat things
that it made Germain pity him. Nevertheless, the
widow laughed as if she admired all the stupid
things he said, and, in that, she gave no proof of
good taste. Germain at first thought that she was
in love with him; but he soon perceived that he was
himself encouraged in a peculiar manner, and that
she wished he would lay himself open more freely.
This was a reason for him to feel and to show himself more cold and more grave. The hour of mass
came, and they all rose from table to go to church.
It was necessary to go as far as Mers, half a league
off, and Germain was so fatigued that he could have
wished to get a good nap beforehand. But he was
not accustomed to miss mass, and he started with
the others.

The roads were covered with people, and the
widow walked with a proud air, escorted by her
three suitors, giving her arm sometimes to one,
sometimes to another, bridling and carrying her head
high. She would have been greatly pleased to produce the fourth to the eyes of the passers by; but
Germain thought it so ridiculous to be trained thus
in company by a petticoat, in the sight of the whole
world, that he kept at a suitable distance, talking
with father Leonard, and finding means of distracting and busying him enough so that they did not
appear to make a part of the band.

H

CHAPTER VII

THE MASTER.

WHEN they reached the village, the widow stopped to wait for them. She was determined to make her entrance with all her suite; but Germain, refusing her this satisfaction, left father Leonard, accosted several persons of his acquaintance, and entered the church by another door. The widow was vexed at it.

After mass, she nevertheless showed herself triumphant on the green, where there was dancing, and opened the dance with her three lovers in succession. Germain watched her motions and thought that she danced well, but affectedly.

"Well!" said Leonard to him, clapping him on the shoulder, "you don't ask my daughter to dance? You are too timid by far."

"I have not danced since I lost my wife," replied the husbandman.

"Well! since you are looking for another, the mourning is at an end in the heart as well as in the dress?"

"That is no reason, father Leonard ; besides, I find myself too old, I don't like to dance any longer."

"Listen," returned Leonard, drawing him to an isolated spot, "you were displeased on entering my house to find the place already surrounded by besiegers, and I see that you are very proud. My daughter is accustomed to be courted, especially during the two years since she finished her mourning, and it was not for her to make advances to you."

"Your daughter has been thinking of marrying these two years and has not yet made up her mind?" said Germain.

"She does not wish to hurry, and she is right. Although she is so sprightly, and perhaps appears to you not to reflect much, she is a woman of great sense, and knows very well what she is about."

"It does not seem so to me," said Germain ingenuously, "for she has three gallants in her suit, and if she knew what she wanted, she would find at least two of them too many, and would request them to stay at home."

"Why so then? You understand nothing about it, Germain. She wishes neither the old man, nor the one eyed, nor the youth, I am almost certain of that : but if she sent them away, it would be believed that she intended to remain a widow and no other would come."

"Oh yes! those fellows serve her as a sign?"

"As you say. Where is the harm?—if it is agreeable to them?"

"Every one to his taste," said Germain.

I see that it would not be yours; but come, we may have an understanding! Suppose that you are preferred, the place could be left free to you."

"Yes, suppose! And until it can be known, how long should I have to stand with my nose in the wind?"

"That depends on yourself, I believe, if you know how to speak and to persuade! Until now my daughter has understood that the best time of her life would be that which she passed in allowing herself to be courted, and she does not feel in a great hurry to become the servant of one man, when she can command several. Thus, so long as the game pleases her, she can divert herself; but if you please more than the game, the game can cease. You have only not to allow yourself to be rebuffed. Come here every Sunday, ask her to dance, let it be known that you put yourself in the ranks, and if she finds you more amiable and better informed than the others, some fine day she will tell you so without doubt."

"Excuse me, father Leonard, your daughter has the right of acting as she judges best, and I have not that of blaming her. In her place, for myself, I should act differently; I should have more frankness and should not make men lose their time, when they have doubtless something better to do than to flutter round a woman who laughs at them. But in fine, if she finds her amusement and happiness in doing so, that is no business of mine. Only it is time that I should tell you one thing which I have been embarrassed to confess to you since this morning, inasmuch as you began by being mistaken respecting my intentions, and did not give me time to reply to you; so that you believe that which is not the case. Know then that I did not come here with the view of asking for your daughter in marriage, but with that of buying from you a yoke of oxen which you mean to drive to the fair next week, and which my father-in-law supposes will suit him."

"I understand, Germain," replied Leonard very quietly. "You have changed your idea on seeing my daughter with her lovers. That is as may please you. It appears that what attracts some repels others, and you have certainly the right to retire since you have not spoken. If you seriously wish to buy my oxen, come and see them in the pasture; we will talk about them, and, whether we make a bargain or not, you will come and dine with us before returning home."

"I do not wish you to incommode yourself," replied Germain, "perhaps you have some business here; as for me, I am tired of looking at the dance and having nothing to do. I will go and see your beasts and meet you by-and-by at your house."

Thereupon Germain slipped away and directed his steps towards the meadow, where Leonard had, in fact, shown him a part of his cattle. It was true that father Maurice wished to buy some, and Germain thought that if he carried back to him a handsome yoke of oxen at a moderate price, he would be more easily forgiven for having voluntarily failed in the object of his journey.

He walked quickly and soon found himself at a short distance from Ormeaux. Then he experienced the need of going to kiss his son and also of again seeing little Marie, though he had lost the hope and driven away the thought of owing his happiness to her. All that he had just seen and heard, that coquettish and vain woman, that father at once crafty and limited, who encouraged his daughter in habits of pride and disloyalty, that city luxury which appeared to him an infraction of the dignity of country manners, that time lost in idle and foolish talk, that household so different from his own, and especially that deep discomfort which the man of the fields experiences when he departs from his industrious habits, all the ennui and confusion he had undergone for several hours, gave Germain the desire to find himself again with his child and his little neighbour. Even if he had not been in love with the latter, he would still have sought her for the purpose of distracting himself and restoring his mind to its accustomed tranquillity.

But he looked in vain in the surrounding meadows; he saw there neither Marie nor Petit-Pierre. Yet it was the hour when the *pastours* were in the fields. There was a large flock not far from him. He asked a young boy who was tending them if those were the sheep of Ormeaux.

"Yes," said the child.

"Are you the shepherd? Do boys tend the woolly beasts of the farms in this place?"

"No, I tend them now because the shepherdess
has gone. She was sick."

"But haven't you a new shepherdess arrived this
morning."

"Oh yes, she has already gone too."

"How, gone! hadn't she a child with her?"

"Yes, a little boy that cried. They both went
away after they had been here two hours."

"Went! where?"

"To the place they came from, apparently. I did
not ask them."

"But why did they go away?" asked Germain,
more and more anxious.

"Dame! how can I know?"

"Was there a misunderstanding about the wages?
still that is a thing ought to have been agreed upon
beforehand!"

"I can't tell you anything about it; I saw them
go in and go out, that's all."

Germain directed his steps to the farm-house and
questioned the husbandman. No one could explain
the fact to him, but it was certain that after having
talked with the farmer, the young girl had gone
away without saying a word, carrying with her the
child, who was crying.

"Did any one maltreat my son?" cried Germain,
whose eyes became inflamed.

"Then it was your son? How did he happen to
be with that little girl? Where do you come from
and what is your name?"

Germain seeing that, according to the custom of

the country, they would answer all his questions by other questions, stamped with impatience and asked to speak with the master.

The master was not there; it was not his custom to remain the whole day when he came to the farm. He had mounted his horse, and had departed, they knew not for which other of his farms.

"But in fine," said Germain, suffering with deep anxiety, "can you not know the reason of that young girl's departure?"

The husbandman exchanged a strange smile with his wife, then he replied that he knew nothing about it, that it was none of his business. All that Germain could learn was, that the young girl and the child had gone in the direction of Fourche. He ran to Fourche; the widow and her lovers had not returned, neither had father Leonard. The maid servant told him that a young girl and a child had come to ask for him, but that, not knowing them, she had not been willing to receive them, and had advised them to go to Mers.

"And why did you refuse to receive them?" said Germain, with some temper. "Then you are very distrustful in this country, when you do not open your door to your neighbour."

"Ah! dame," replied the maid servant, "in a rich house like this, we have reason to keep a good guard! I am responsible for everything when the masters are out, and I cannot open to chance comers."

"It is an ugly custom," said Germain, "and I

should much prefer to be poor than to live like
that in constant fear. Good bye, girl! good bye to
your miserable country!"

He made inquiries at the neighbouring houses.
The people had seen the shepherdess and child. As
the little one had left Belair unexpectedly, without
dressing, with his blouse somewhat torn and his
little lamb-skin on his shoulders; as little Marie was
also, and for a good reason, quite poorly dressed at
all times, they had taken them for beggars. They
had offered them bread. The young girl had accepted
a piece for the child who was hungry; then she had
departed very hastily with him and gained the wood.

Germain reflected a moment; then he asked if the
farmer of Ormeaux had not come to Fourche.

"Yes," he was answered: "he passed on horseback, a few minutes after that little girl."

"Was he running after her?"

"Ah! you know him then?" said the tavern
keeper of the place, to whom he addressed himself;
" yes, certainly, he is a devil of a fellow for running
after girls. But I don't believe he caught that one
—though, after all, if he had seen her——"

"That's enough, thank you!" said Germain. And
he flew rather than ran to Leonard's stables. He
threw his pack-saddle on the Grise, leaped upon it,
and started at full gallop in the direction of the wood
of Chanteloube.

His heart bounded with anxiety and anger, and
the sweat poured from his forehead. He brought
blood from the sides of the Grise, who, seeing her-

self on the road to her stable, did not require much urging to make her run.

Germain soon found himself at the spot where he had passed the night on the bank of the pool. The fire was still smoking; an old woman was gathering the remains of the supply of dead wood which little Marie had heaped up there. Germain stopped to question her. She was deaf, and misunderstanding his interrogations—

"Yes, my boy," said she, "this is the Devil's Pool. It is a bad place, and you must not come near it without throwing three stones into it with your left hand, while you make the sign of the cross with your right. That drives away spirits. Otherwise misfortunes happen to those who go round it."

"I am not speaking to you of that," said Germain, going near to her and shouting loud enough to split his head. "Have you not seen pass in the wood a girl and a child?"

"Yes," said the old woman, "a little child was drowned in it."

Germain shuddered from head to foot; but happily the old woman added:

"That was a long while ago; in memory of the accident a beautiful cross was planted here; but in a very stormy night, the bad spirits threw it into the water. You can see an end of it still. If any one should have the misfortune to stop here at night, he would be very sure not to be able to get out before day. He might walk, and walk, all he could; he

might travel two hundred leagues in the wood, and
always find himself again in the same place."

The husbandman's imagination was struck by
what he heard, in spite of himself; and the idea of
the misfortune that must needs happen, in order to
justify completely the old woman's assertions, took
such full possession of his head that he felt cold in
his whole body. In despair of obtaining any further
information, he remounted his horse, and again began to ride through the wood, calling Pierre with
all his strength, whistling, cracking his whip, break-
ing the branches in order to fill the forest with the
noise of his passage, listening afterwards if any
voice replied to him; but he heard only the bells of
the cows scattered through the thicket, and the wild
cry of the hogs quarrelling for the acorns.

At last Germain heard behind him the noise of a
horse that was following his steps, and a man between two ages, brown, stout, and in a half citizen's
dress, cried out to him to stop. Germain had never
seen the farmer of Ormeaux: but an instinct of rage
made him judge at once that this was he. He turned
back, and measuring him from head to feet, waited
for what he had to say.

"Have you not seen a young girl of fifteen or sixteen years old pass this way with a little boy?" said
the farmer, affecting an air of indifference, though
he was visibly excited.

"And what do you want of her?" replied Germain, without seeking to disguise his anger.

"I might tell you that that is none of your busi-

ness, comrade ; but as I have no reasons for conceal-
ing it, I will tell you that she is a shepherdess whom
I had hired for the year without knowing her. When
I saw her arrive, she seemed to me too young and
too weak for the work of the farm. I have declined
her services ; but I wished to pay the expenses of
her little journey, and she went away vexed while I
had my back turned. She was in such a hurry that
she even forgot a part of her things and her purse,
which does not contain much, you may be sure ; a
few sous, probably ! But, in fine, as I had to pass
this way, I thought I would meet her and give her
what she left behind, and what I owe her."

Germain was too honest a soul not to hesitate on
hearing this story, if not very probable, at least possible. He fixed a piercing eye upon the farmer, who
bore this investigation with a great deal of impu-
dence or of candour.

"I wish to have my heart clear," said Germain to
himself, and restraining his agitation :

"She is a girl from our place," said he, "I know
ner, she must be hereabouts ; we will go on together ; we shall find her without doubt."

"You are right," said the farmer, "let us go on ;
and yet, if we do not find her at the end of the
avenue, I shall give her up, for I must be on my way
to Ardentes."

"Oh!" thought the husbandman, "I shall not
leave you even should I have to turn with you
twenty-four hours round the Devil's Pool."

"Stop," said Germain suddenly, fixing his eyes

upon a tuft of furze which was singularly agitated. "Hallo! ho! Petit-Pierre! is that you, my child?"

The child, recognising his father's voice, came out from the furze, leaping like a goat; but when he saw him in company with the farmer, he stopped as if frightened, and remained undecided.

"Come, my Pierre, come, it is I!" cried the husbandman, hastening towards him, and leaping down from his horse to take him in his arms; "and where is little Marie?"

"She is hiding in there, because she is afraid of that ugly black man; and I too!"

"Oh! you may be quiet, I am there. Marie, Marie! It is I!"

Marie came out crawling, and as soon as she saw Germain, whom the farmer followed close behind, she ran to throw herself into his arms, and, fastening to him as a daughter to her father:

"Ah! my brave Germain," said she to him, "you will defend me, I am not afraid with you."

Germain felt a shiver. He looked at Marie; she was pale; her clothes were torn by the thorns among which she had run, seeking a covert, like a doe tracked by the hunters. But there was neither shame nor despair in her face.

"Your master wishes to speak to you," said he to her, still observing her features.

"My master!" said she proudly, "that man is not my master, and never will be. It is you, Germain, who are my master! I wish you to carry me back with you. I will serve you for nothing."

The farmer advanced, pretending a little impatience.

"Hey! little one," said he, "you forgot at our place something which I have brought for you."

"Not so, sir," replied little Marie, "I have forgotten nothing, and I have nothing to ask of you."

"Listen a little this way," returned the farmer; "I have something to say to you, I really have! Come, don't be afraid, only two words!"

"You may say them out aloud; I have no secrets with you."

"Come and take your money at least!"

"My money; you owe me nothing, thank God!"

"I thought so," said Germain in a half voice; "but no matter, Marie; listen to what he has to say; for my part, I am curious to know; you will tell me afterwards, I have my reasons for that. Go to the side of the house, I will not lose you from my sight."

Marie made three steps towards the farmer, who said to her, leaning over the pommel of his saddle and lowering his voice:

"Little one, here is a handsome louis d'or for you; you will say nothing, do you understand? I shall say that I found you too weak for the work of my farm. And let there be no more talk of that! I shall pass again near your house one of these days, and if you have said nothing, I will give you something more; and then, if you are more reasonable, you have only to tell me so, and I will take you back to my house, or else I will come and talk with you in the field at dusk. What present do you wish me to bring you?"

"This, sir, is the present that I make to you, my-self," replied little Marie in a loud voice, throwing his louis d'or into his face, and with some force. "I thank you a great deal, and beg of you, when you intend to pass near our house, to give me notice. All the boys of my place will go to receive you, be-cause with us they love very much the citizens who wish to speak improperly to poor girls. You will see that they will expect you."

"You are a liar and a foolish talker," said the farmer angered, while he raised his stick with a threatening air; "you would wish to make people believe that which is not; but you will not get any money from me: girls like you are well known."

Marie had drawn back frightened; but Germain had rushed forward to the farmer's bridle, and forcibly shaking it :

"It is understood, now," said he, "and we see clearly enough what he wants. Get down, my man; get down! and let us talk together."

The farmer had no desire to engage in the conver-sation; he spurred his horse to clear him, and tried to strike the husbandman's hands with his stick, in order to make him let go; but Germain avoided the blow, and taking him by the leg, unhorsed him and threw him on the fern, where he got him down, though the farmer had regained his feet and defended himself vigorously. When he had him under him

"Man of little heart," said Germain to him, "I could beat you black and blue, if I wished! but I do not like to do an injury; and besides, no correction would amend your conscience. Nevertheless, you will not go from here until you have asked this young girl's pardon on your knees."

The farmer, who was acquainted with this kind of affairs, wished to treat the thing as a joke. He pretended that his fault was not a serious one, since it consisted only in words, and that he was very willing to ask pardon for it, on condition that he might kiss the girl, that they should go together and drink a pint of wine at the nearest tavern, and then separate good friends.

"You disgust me," replied Germain, pushing his face against the ground, "and I am in a hurry to lose sight of your wicked looks. There, blush if you can, and try to take the road of the shame-faced,* when you pass near our house."

He picked up the holly stick of the farmer, broke across his knee, in order to show him the strength of his fists, and threw the pieces to a distance from him with contempt.

Then, taking his son in one hand, and little Marie in the other, he withdrew, trembling all over with indignation.

---

* This is the road which turns from the principal street at the entrance of the villages, and runs round them on the outside. It is supposed that persons who fear to receive some deserved affront, take it to avoid being seen.

CHAPTER VIII.

MOTHER MAURICE.

In a quarter of an hour they had cleared the heath, they were trotting on the highway, and the Grise was whinnying at every object of her acquaintance. Petit-Pierre related to his father all that he had been able to understand of what had taken place.

"When we arrived," said he, "that *man there* came to speak to *my Marie*, in the sheep barn, where we had gone at once to see the handsome sheep. As for me, I had climbed up into the manger to play, and that *man there* didn't see me. Then he said 'how do you do?' to *my Marie*, and he kissed her."

"You let him kiss you, Marie!" said Germain, trembling all over with anger.

"I thought it was an honest thing—a custom of the place with new comers, as, at your house, the grandmother kisses the young girls who enter her service, to let them see that she adopts them, and that she will be as a mother to them."

"And so then," resumed Petit-Pierre, who was proud to have an adventure to relate, "that *man*

I

there said something ugly to you, something that you told me never to repeat, and not to recollect: so I forgot it very quickly. But if my father wishes me to tell him what it was——"

"No, no, Pierre, I don't want to hear it, and I wish that you would never recollect it."

"In that case, I will forget it again," resumed the child. "And so then, that *man there* seemed to be put out, because *my Marie* told him she would go away. He told her he would give her everything she wanted, a hundred francs! and *my Marie* got put out too; then he came against her, as if he would do her some harm. I was frightened, and I ran to *my Marie*, crying. Then that *man there* said:

"'What is that? Where does that child come from? Put him out of doors.'

"And he lifted up his stick to beat me. But *my Marie* prevented him, and she said:

"'We will talk by and by, sir; now I must carry this child to Fourche, and then I will come back.'

"And as soon as he had gone out of the sheep-barn, *my Marie* said to me:

"'Let us run, my Pierre, let us go away from here as quick as we can; for that man is wicked, and he will only do us harm.'

"Then we passed behind the barns, we crossed a little field, and we went to Fourche after you. But you were not there; and they were not willing to let us wait for you. And then that *man there*, who was mounted on his black horse, came behind us; and we ran off still further; and then we went to hide ourselves in the woods. And then, he came there too ; and when we heard him coming, we hid ourselves. And then, when he had passed, we began to run again to go home ; and then at last you came, and you found us, and that is how it all happened. Isn't it so, *my Marie*, have I forgotten anything ?"

"No, my Pierre, and all that is the truth. Now, Germain, you will bear witness for me, and you will tell everybody at home, that if I could not stay, it was not for want of courage and desire to work."

"And you, Marie," said Germain, "I will beg you to ask yourself if, when one has to defend a woman and to punish an insolent fellow, a man of twenty-eight is too old? I should really like to know if Bastien, or any other pretty boy, rich by ten years less of age than me, would not have been crushed by that *man there*, as Petit-Pierre says. What do you think about it ?"

"I think, Germain, that you have rendered me a great service, and that I shall thank you for it my whole life."

"Is that all ?"

"My little papa," said the child, "I have not thought to say to little Marie what I promised you; but I will say it to her at the house, and I will say it to my grandmother too."

This promise of his child at last made Germain think. He had now to come to an explanation with his relatives, and while telling them his objections against the widow Guerin, not to tell them what other ideas had predisposed him to so much clear-sightedness and severity. When one is happy and proud, the courage to make one's happiness accepted by others appears easy; but to be repelled on the one hand, and blamed on the other, does not constitute a very agreeable situation.

Fortunately, little Pierre was asleep when they reached the farm, and Germain deposited him on his bed without waking him. Then he entered into all the explanations he could give. Father Maurice, seated on his three-legged stool at the entrance of the house, listened to him gravely, and, although he was dissatisfied with the result of this journey, when Germain, in relating the widow's system of coquetry, asked his father-in-law if he had time to go and pay his court the fifty-two Sundays in the year, to risk being dismissed at the end, the father-in-law replied, bowing his head in token of assent:

"You were not wrong, Germain, that could not be."

And afterwards, when Germain related how he had been compelled to bring back little Marie as quickly as possible, in order to withdraw her from the insults, perhaps from the violence, of an unworthy master, father Maurice again approved with his head, saying:

"You were not wrong, Germain: that was your duty."

When Germain had finished his recital, and given all his reasons, the father-in-law and mother-in-law simultaneously drew a deep sigh of resignation, as they looked at each other. Then the head of the family rose, saying:

"Well! the will of God be done! Friendship cannot be commanded!"

"Come and get your supper, Germain," said the mother-in-law. "It is unfortunate that the arrangement could not be made; but God did not will it should be, as it appears. We must look elsewhere."

"Yes," added the old man, "as my wife says, we will look elsewhere."

There was no further talk in the house; and when, the next day, little Pierre rose with the larks at dawn, being no longer excited by the extraordinary events of the preceding days, he fell again into the usual apathy of little peasants of his age, forgot all that had been running through his head, and no longer thought of anything but sporting with his brother and sister, and *playing man* with the oxen and horses.

Germain tried to forget also, by applying himself anew to work; but he became so sad and absent that everybody remarked it. He did not speak to little Marie; he did not even look at her; and yet, if any one had asked him in what field she was, by what road she had gone, there was not an hour of the day in which he could not have told, had he been willing to answer. He had not dared to ask his parents to receive her on the farm during the winter, and yet he knew very well that she must suffer from poverty. But she did not suffer: mother Guillette could never understand how her little supply of wood did not diminish, and how her shed was full in the morning when she had almost emptied it the evening before. It was the same with the wheat and the potatoes. Somebody passed by the opening of the granary and emptied a bag upon the floor without awakening any one and without leaving any traces. The old woman was at once anxious and delighted; she desired her daughter not to speak of it, saying that if the neighbours should come to know what a miracle was performed at her house, she would be taken for a witch. She really thought that the devil had something to do with it, but she was in no hurry to quarrel with him by calling the exorcisms of the curate upon the house; she said to herself that it would be time enough when Satan came to ask for her soul in return for his benefits.

Little Marie understood the truth better, but she did not dare to speak of it to Germain, for fear of seeing him return to his notion of marriage; and with him she pretended to perceive nothing.

One day mother Maurice, finding herself alone with Germain in the orchard, said to him in a friendly tone:

"My poor son-in-law, I think that you are not well. You do not eat so well as usual, you no longer laugh, and you talk less and less. Has any one of our family or ourselves, without knowing and without wishing it, given you pain?"

"No, Mother," replied Germain, "you have always been as good to me as the mother who brought me into this world, and I should be very ungrateful if I complained of you, or of your husband, or of any one in the family."

"In that case, my child, it is the grief for the loss of your wife that comes back upon you. Instead of going away with time, your trouble grows worse. and you must absolutely do what your father-in-law very wisely advised you. You must marry again."

"Yes, mother, that would also be my idea, but the women whom you advised me to ask do not suit me. When I see them, instead of forgetting my Catherine, I think of her still more."

"Apparently, Germain, that is because we have not known how to guess your taste. Thus you must help us by telling us the truth. Without doubt there is somewhere a woman who is made for you, for the good God never makes any one without reserving his happiness for him in another person. If, therefore, you know where to take her, that woman whom you must needs have, take her; and whether she be handsome or ugly, young or old, rich or poor, we have decided, my old man and me, to give you our consent; for we are tired with seeing you sad, and we cannot live tranquil if you are not so."

"My mother, you are as good as the good God, and my father equally," replied Germain; "but your compassion can give no remedy to my sorrows; the girl whom I should like to have does not like me."

"Then she must be too young for you? It is unreasonable in you to be attached to a young person."

"Well! yes, good mother, I am so foolish as to be attached to a young person, and I blame myself for it. I do my best not to think about her; but whether I am at work or resting, whether I am at mass or in my bed, with my children or with you, I think of her always, and can think of nothing else."

"Then it is like a spell that has been cast upon you, Germain? There is but one remedy, which is, that the girl should change her idea and listen to you. It is therefore necessary that I should take it in hand, and that I should see if it is possible. You must tell me where she is, and what is her name."

"Alas! my dear mother, I do not dare to," said Germain, "because you will certainly laugh at me."

"I shall not laugh at you, Germain, because you are in trouble, and I do not wish to increase it. Can it be Fanchette?"

"No, mother, it is not."

"Or Rosette?"

"No."

"Tell me then, for I shall not stop, if I must name all the girls in the country."

Germain bowed his head and could not make up his mind to answer.

"Well!" said mother Maurice, "I will let you alone for to-day, Germain; perhaps to-morrow you will be more confiding with me, or perhaps your sister-in-law will be more skilful in questioning you."

And she took up her basket to go and spread her linen on the bushes.

Germain acted like children who decide when they see that people will no longer pay attention to them. He followed his mother-in-law, and at last tremblingly named to her *mother Guillette's little Marie.*

Great was mother Maurice's surprise; it was the last girl she would have thought of. But she had the delicacy not to cry out and to make her comments mentally. Then, seeing that her silence overpowered Germain, she held out her basket to him saying:

"Come, is that a reason for not helping me in my work? Take this load and come and talk with me. Have you reflected well, Germain? are you entirely decided?"

"Alas! my dear mother, it is not in that way we must talk. I should be decided if I could succeed: but as I shall not be listened to, I am only decided to cure myself if I can do it."

"And if you cannot?"

"Everything has its end, mother Maurice; when the horse is too heavily loaded, he falls; and when the ox has nothing to eat, he dies."

"That is to say that you will die, if you do not succeed? God forbid, Germain! I do not like to have such a man as you say such things, for when he says them he thinks them. You have great courage, and weakness is dangerous in strong people. Come, take hope. I cannot conceive that a girl in deep poverty, and to whom you do great honour by asking her, can refuse you."

"Nevertheless that is the truth, sne does refuse me."

"And what reasons does she give you for it"

"That you have always done her good, that her family owes a great deal to your's, and that she does not wish to displease you by preventing me from making a rich marriage."

"If she says that, she gives proof of good feelings, and it is honest on her part. But in telling you that, Germain, she does not cure you, for she doubtless tells you that she loves you, and that she would marry you if we were willing."

"That's the worst of it, she tells me that her heart is not drawn towards me."

"If she says what she does not think in order the better to withdraw you from her, she is a child who deserves that we should love her, and that we should pass over her youth for the sake of her being so very reasonable."

"Yes," said Germain, struck with a hope he had not yet conceived; "that would be very wise and very *comme il faut* on her part, would it not? but if she is so reasonable, I fear it is because I do not please her.

"Germain," said mother Maurice, "you will promise me that you will keep quiet the whole week, that you will not torment yourself, that you will eat, sleep, and be gay as before. As for me, I will talk with my old man, and if I make him consent, then you can learn the real feelings of the girl respecting you."

Germain promised, and the week passed without father Maurice saying a word to him in particular, or appearing to imagine anything. The husbandman tried to appear tranquil, but he was always more pale and more tormented.

At last, Sunday morning, on coming out from mass, his mother-in-law asked him what he had obtained from his beloved since the conversation in the orchard.

"Why, nothing at all," replied he, "I have not spoken to her."

"How then do you expect to persuade her, if you do not speak to her?"

"I have spoken to her only once," replied Germain. "It was when we went together to Fourche; and since that time I have not said a single word to her. Her refusal gave me so much pain, that I prefer not to hear her begin again to tell me that she does not love me."

"Well, my son, you must speak to her now; your father-in-law authorizes you to do so. Go, have it decided! I tell you so, and if it is necessary, I wish you to do it; for you cannot remain in such a doubt."

Germain obeyed. He arrived at the Guillette's, with his head bowed down and an oppressed manner. Little Marie was alone, at the corner of the fire, so pensive that she did not hear Germain enter. When she saw him before her, she started with surprise on her chair and became quite red.

"Little Marie," said he, seating himself by her

side, I come to trouble you and to weary you, I know it very well: but *the man and woman of our house*" (designating thus the heads of the family, according to custom,) "wish me to speak to you, and to ask you to marry me. You do not wish to, do you? I expect it."

"Germain," replied Marie, "then it is decided that you do love me?"

"That plagues you, I know, but it is not my fault; if you could change your mind, I should be too happy, and doubtless I do not deserve that it should be so. Come, look at me, Marie, am I then very horrible?"

"No, Germain," replied she smiling, "you are handsomer than I am."

"Do not laugh at me, Marie; look at me with indulgence. I have not lost a tooth or a hair. My eyes tell you that I love you. Look into my eyes once, it is written there, and every girl knows how to read that writing."

Marie looked into Germain's eye with her cheerful assurance; then she suddenly turned away her head and began to tremble.

"Ah! *mon Dieu!* I frighten you," said Germain; "do not fear me, I beg of you, that pains me too much. I will not say any bad words to you, not I; I will not kiss you in spite of yourself, and when you wish me to go, you have only to point to the door. Come, must I go in order that you may stop trembling?"

Marie extended her hand to the husbandman, but

without turning her head, which was bowed towards
the hearth, and without saying a word.

"I understand," said Germain; "you pity me,
you are good, you are sorry to make me unhappy;
but can you not love me?"

"Why do you say these things to me, Germain?"
replied little Marie at last, "do you wish to make
me cry?"

"Poor little girl, you have a good heart, I know;
but you do not love me, and you hide your face
because you fear to let me see your displeasure and
your repugnance. And I, I dare not even press
your hand. In the wood, when my son was asleep,
and you were asleep too, I came near kissing you
very softly. But I should have died of shame rather
than ask you, and I suffered as much in that night
as a man who was burning at a slow fire. Since
that time I have dreamt of you every night. Ah!
how I kissed you, Marie! But you, during that
time, you slept without dreaming. And now, do
you know what I think? I think that if you should
turn round and look at me with the eyes that I have
for you, and should bring your face near to mine, I
should fall dead with joy. And you, you think that
if such a thing should happen, you would die with
anger and shame."

Germain spoke as in a dream, without understand-
ng what he said.

Little Marie still trembled; but, as he trembled
still more, he no longer perceived it. Suddenly she
turned round; her face was bathed in tears, and she

looked at him with a reproachful air. The poor husbandman thought that this was the last blow, and, without waiting for his sentence, rose to depart. But the young girl stopped him by encircling him with both her arms, and hiding her head in his bosom:

"Ah! Germain," said she sobbing, "did you not guess that I loved you?"

Germain would have become crazy, if his son, who was looking for him and who entered the hut at full gallop on a stick, with his little sister behind him, whipping the imaginary courser with a willow switch, had not recalled him to himself. He raised him in his arms and placing him in those of his betrothed:

"Here," said he to her, "you have made more than one person happy by loving me."

FANCHETTE.

From Blaise Bonnin, to Claude Germain.

This comes, my dear godfather, to thank you for
your letter and to give you news of our health. As
for us, we are pretty well, thank God; and the fever
has spared all our flock, notwithstanding the unhealthy summer, which has frightened the poor, and
made the doctors' pockets sing for joy. The young
ones have borne it no worse than the older, and
grandmother, your "*Gossip,*"* as you call her,
excepting that she does not hear so well as she did,
is yet quite willing to live on, thanks to a good God.
The harvest has not been so bad as one might have
feared; but as for the vintage, it is no use to talk of
eight oxen, neither of six, of four, nor even of two,
to carry it home, Jarvais' ass might very well
manage it in a basket. As for drinking, one's throat
may go dry; however, that is better than having
one's stomach pinched for want of bread. But, bad
is the best in such a case; and with one thing or

* "Commere."

another, the poor may make their minds up that they have not done with suffering yet awhile.

"But that is easy enough to say for those who do not feel the worst of it. Some few may preach temperance, and M. le Cure, whose cellar is not empty, will have plenty to say on that subject, but the greater number declare that when the wine is out, the courage fails, and strength relaxes. And besides, that is not the worst of the matter. Those who are strong enough manage to struggle on, and if they do break down, that is their own business, as people say. Those who do not wish to over-task their limbs, and who like to rejoice their hearts a little on Sundays (and it seems to me there are many of this sort, who have not deserved hanging for en-joying a little of the country wine hereabouts) these, I say, will comprehend nothing of M. le Cure's reasons, and will go to the Holly-bush as usual. Do you think godfather, that the taverns will be deserted this year, that the spits will turn rusty, and that the spiders may weave their nets in the wine casks? Nothing of the kind! There will be as much wine as usual, and perhaps no dearer than usual; for every one must still go there; the public-house can no more do without the beggar's pence, than the beggar can do without the *piquette** of the public house. Let us see what sort of piquette it will be, and what wine will sparkle in our stone cups : Issoudun is not frozen up, and Issoudun will

* Small acid wine.

send us her strong black wines, which make our peasantry dull and heavy headed, accustomed as they are to their lively claret. It is true the publicans will soon arrange all that, and out of one tun of Issoudun wine they will make at least ten; the other parts will come from the druggist, the colour will be good, *headiness* will not be wanting. Nobody will be the loser, except that the general health will be injured, and all sorts of diseases will inundate us, like a swarm of flies, by the return of spring.

You will tell me, that the hospital will do its duty, that is to say, ensure the salvation of those pious souls who lay up good works here as a rent-charge for Paradise hereafter. You, who have farmed, for fifteen years, a portion of the hospital lands, you know, godfather, that there are set apart for the relief of the poor, eighteen hundred or two th and pistoles at least. Allow fifteen thousand livres, for a year's income, that seems ample to assist the most needy of the canton. But if you ask me what necessitous persons ever *have* been assisted by this revenue of the hospital, I should be considerably puzzled to tell you. The hospital has always its six beds, neither more nor less. With but one thousand pistoles could they not keep up at least twenty beds? That would be something; then there would remain enough of the aforesaid revenue to set up a House of Refuge, to support the three nuns, who are considered as *sisters of charity*, even to build a little, since the Administration makes such a point of having its six beds in a palace, and to pay M. le

K

Cure well for his masses, as he will not say them, though for the sick, under a crown. Everything is dear enough now, and even the priests do not keep to their tariff.

But to return to the hospital: we had the greatest trouble to get that poor devil, Daudet, admitted although he came back from the army with his chest dreadfully crushed by the horses' feet in a manœuvre. They would have nothin g to do with him, but sent him about, from Herod to Pilate, and we had to bring Cross and Banner to prevent their turning him into the street. But that is nothing of consequence. A man who cannot work for his living, because his ribs are broken, is not worth talking about of course. But we have seen something still better than this; and since you ask me about that story of a lost child, w   a Lorrain has been puzzling you with; and a.so. godfather, as you are in a manner belonging to the hospital, and are always interested in the underhand dealings there, I will give you a full history of the affair.

Last March, just at seed-time, a girl of some fifteen years of age, rather pretty, and wretchedly clad, was found, as though dropped from the sky, just to the right of the meadow Burat, two steps from the town She had been wandering about for three days, without any one's knowing to whom she belonged, and without her knowing herself, poor soul. It should seem that her mother could neither find her in bread, nor furnish her with speech to ask for it. The poor thing can reason about as much as my billhook;

has no more knowledge than a kid, and is as dumb
as any stone; she may hear, but cannot say a word;
appears to have no remembrance of yesterday, and
to take no thought of the morrow. In fact she is
good for nothing, and any one who is thinking only
of this life, had better find a quail in his field than
an innocent like this at his door. And yet she is not
wicked, the poor child, she has done no wrong, she
would not be able to do any. How can she deserve
death? Whose place is it to do away with all that
may be useless on this earth? It is not mine, I should
have too much work upon my hands.

If this poor creature has done nothing to deserve
death, then she has a right to life. Now follow my
idea, godfather. That is to say, she has a right to
food, clothing, shelter, to care, in short, to *Charity.*
If the state has no resources for idiots or infirm
people, then they must fall a dead weight on us,
poor as we are. For we cannot let them perish at
our threshold; the fact of the great disgrace, that
such a thing would bring upon us, shows also its
wickedness. But we have trouble enough to make
both ends meet in our best times, and the greatest
number amongst us cannot even do that. When we
can manage to keep our old people, our sick, and
our infirm poor amongst us, it is a sign that we are
rather rich. But when we cannot! What is to be
done then? What is to become of them? There
either is a government or there is not. I demand an
answer to this question, and I, Blaise Bonnin, have
a right to understand what the law *is* upon this

point.   I am the Mayor's Assistant for the Commune, and I hope to be its Mayor some day or other.
Well, they tell me there are funds set aside by the
Department for the support of those who cannot
support tnemselves.   They are far from rich apparently, but at any rate, there are such funds.   Let
them be used then.   And if they are not made use
of, or if they are managed by people who either do
not know how, or will not administer them properly,
to whom are we to complain? from whom must we
demand justice?

My wife, who is no fool, as you know, and who
has a superb* heart, said to me, when we saw this
poor girl with neither house nor home, wandering
about, that if the government did not interfere, she,
Jacquette, would, and put the government to shame,
by taking the child under her own care, even if she
must water the soup for her own children.''

"Wait a bit, wife," said I, "if this goes on so, of
course we must do it, but it cannot continue."

"And whilst we are waiting," said Jacquette,
" God knows what may happen to a poor young
thing like that, who begins to be worth looking at,
and who might easily go wrong, not knowing her
right hand from her left."

So I went to look for the little one, but a young
physician of the hospital who was passing by, found
her in the midst of a crowd of children, who were
playing with her, as with a bundle of rags, and teaz-

---

* Provincialism for excellent, generous.

ing her cruelly to make her speak. The poor creature could do nothing but weep, and murmur a few
broken words, which no one could understand better
than a sheep's bleating. The good young man made
some enquiries about her, and took her to the hospital. Of course, you think they take her in, comfort her and console her? Nothing of the sort. A
lost child, is nevertheless of some consequence, and
I think if I had nothing else to do in this world but
to pray to God, and to serve the poor, I would wel-
come all that God might send me. Not so—they
refuse the child. " *It* is too stupid, too neglected, it
wants too much care bestowed upon it, it is no affair
of ours, we have nothing to do with idiots, we do
not take in vagabonds. Do you take the hospital
for a mad house, or a mendicity depot? A pretty
imposition upon us indeed!"

The doctor insists. He gives a certificate of sick-
ness to the child; and behold Fanchette, (they gave
her this name) taken into the hospital somewhat
against every body's will. She was delighted to be
there, and employed herself as much as her feeble
intelligence allowed her. She was very gentle, and
was quite happy playing with the other little girls,
who were confided to the nuns' care. These children loved, and never tormented her. When the
nuns clothed her in the dress of a little sister of
charity, she thought herself as grand as a queen;
and when she was taken to mass, she stared about,
and thought it so fine, that she seemed to wish the
end might never come. I do not know if any rule

in the hospital forbade them to keep this most unfortunate of God's creatures; but if it had been an
abuse of power to keep her, it is my belief that there
are many worse abuses than this in the world, and
perhaps even in the hospital itself. However, what
was sure, was, they would not keep her. The Prefect was written to, and he set apart from the funds
destined for the support of the lunatics of the department, a small sum to pay for Fanchette's board
and lodging under the care of the hospital. They
put Fanchette into the hands of one of those women
who take foundlings to look after them. But how
was Fanchette to know that it was her duty to stay
there? she understood nothing about it. She de-
camped after the first hour, and went to seek her
little play-fellows, the good sisters, and the beautiful
high mass. They sent her back to the old woman,
but Fanchette was off again to the hospital. Again
they sent her back—once, twice, thrice, four times,
perhaps even oftener, but it was all of no use, Fanchette ran to the hospital just as others run away
from it. They would be forced to keep her entirely.

"Now," said the Lady Superior, "what shall
we do with this Fanchette who is so much in our
way?"

"Oh," said one, "it is very easy, she is a child
lost expressly by somebody at the hospital gates; it
is an awkward present they have sent us."

"It is a trick played us by some other congrega-
tion," said another.

"Well then," rejoined the orator of the council,

(the strongest head among them be sure), "we must put her where we found her, on the wayside. Some one had lost her, let *us* lose her too. She came from the good God let her return to the good God."

"Amen," said the excellent sister.

No sooner said than done.

"Fanchette, would you like to go to mass?"

Fanchette jumps for joy.

"Come then, put your Sunday cap on. The servant will take you."

Who was pleased if Fanchette was not? It was broad daylight, they could not lose her in the sight and knowledge of every one. They made her traverse the city, and the woman who conducted her, not meaning any harm perhaps, said to her, as they passed by houses where she knew any one; "Now Fanchette, say good bye to Margaret, say good bye to Catherine."

Fanchette, whom every thing pleased, made signs with head and hand, the best she could do, and went her way to mass, proud enough of having a cap on, and not tormenting herself to know why the church of the Capuchins was so far off. But the little girls at their house doors, for there always is a providence watching evil doers, said, "What, is Fanchette going away? Adieu, Fanchette, a happy journey to you."

At the end of the town, Thomas Desroys, the conducter of the *patache* from Aubusson, received

Fanchette, who mounted without any mistrust, better pleased still at going to mass in a carriage.

"But all this is rather odd," said Thomas Desroys to himself, "losing a child in this manner. Some one gave me fifty sous yesterday to lose a dog, and to day they give me a hundred to lose a child. If one half the town would agree with me to lose the other half, that would be a capital affair for me."

When night had fallen, Thomas Desroys, faithful to his orders, stopped his patache at Chaussidout, a desert place, in La Marche, about six miles from Aubusson.

"Now, Fanchette here is the mass; get down quickly that you may see the priests go by."

Fanchette trustingly dismounts. Thomas Desroys takes his seat again, whips his horses, and leaves Fanchette alone, in the middle of the night, on a high road, without a penny, but with her fifteen years, without a tongue to speak, but with her poor eyes to weep.

After some little time, the young doctor, who had first picked up the poor innocent, is surprised at not seeing her any where, and asks what is become of her.

"She is here, she is there, you will see her soon, some other day."

However, sometime or other, it must come out. The little girls in the street of the Capuchins, remember having said good bye to Fanchette, and it is not very easy to keep little girls from talking. And besides the servant's conscience perhaps was

not quite tranquil, nor Thomas Desroys' either. All
was acknowledged, and the nuns themselves, thinking Fanchette was thoroughly lost now, made no
difficulty of owning everything.

Just at this stage of the affair, our mayor, who is,
as you know also our deputy, came back from Paris,
Informed by the public outcry, he wished to question and know who were the guilty ones. No one
cared much to reply; for they were beginning to
see, that it is not so fine a deed to lose a child upon
a highway, and that if a poor person had played a
trick of this sort, the galleys would soon be talked
of for him, to teach him how to conduct himself.
But the mayor insists, and seeks for proofs. Ar
enquiry is instituted, and the result is that Thomas
Desroys had received from his superiors, the order
to lose a little girl; that the said superiors, the post-
masters, and diligence contractors, had given this
order at the request of the Lady Superior of the
hospital, who had herself received it from the most
influential members of the Council of Administration. The people at the diligence office, say, they
thought the commission disagreeable, but that the
Lady Superior did away with their scruples by telling them the girl should not be inscribed on their
list of travellers. The Lady Superior says she
would not have undertaken the affair, but that the
Administrator had strongly recommended it. The
other members of the Council say that it is nonsense,
that it is quite ridiculous to make a fuss about such
a trifling matter, that it will cause a scandal, and
throw odium upon very respectable people, that is

to say upon rich and influential people, and that
they are resolved to keep silence about it, for the
sake of good morals and the greater glory of God.
The councellor, the originator of the idea, pretends
that they outrage and calumniate him. He threatens
to make a complaint, and to bring dishonour upon
the mayoralty. Our mayor cares little about that,
and pursues the enquiry. There is only Thomas
Desroys who makes no ceremony about the matter
—he had fifty sous more than for the dog he lost.
With one hand, the mayor acts for the sake of justice,
and one may well say, without fear of exaggeration,
that it is God's justice which is in question in this
affair; and with the other hand he seeks Fanchette;
but Fanchette has been this time so thoroughly lost,
that for nearly three months no one has had any
news of her. No one at Aubusson has heard anything of her. They tell us from all parts, that they
can hear no more of Fanchette than of the Prosecution so well deserved by the hospital. The Attorney-
General and the Sub-Prefect have received the Complaint, but take no notice of it. All the respectable
people of the place (you know, godfather, that since
the revolution, the rich people and the place-men
take this name) say that this thing must be hushed
up,—oh! if you, or I, or neighbour Jarvois, or Mar-
casse, had done only half as much, there would not
have been a sufficiency of gendarmes, gaolers, wit-
nesses, judges, laws, nor prisons, to seize upon, condemn and punish us. I do not say that it would
have been ill done, but it is certainly not well done
to be so over easy with some and so sharp after

others. I am no backbiter, I wish no ill to any one,
and I know that even punishing the wicked will not
restore honour or life to those who have suffered
from their deeds; but I cannot help having my head
and heart both fuller than is agreeable, when I hear
it said that we ought to hide the faults of those who
have no conscience. If justice is not to touch them,
well, all in good time, but we cannot be hindered,
from blaming them, and *mordienne!* to my very last
hour will I condemn those who lose a child just as
they would a dog. As for Fanchette, will God have
had more pity for her than the hospital had? It is
said that God tempers the wind to the shorn lamb.
But at night, and on those wild heaths, there are
numbers of marshy places where a child without a
pennyworth of knowledge might easily be drowned.
Without considering what worse things might happen upon the high roads. There are plenty of evil-
disposed persons, who, meeting a girl of fifteen quite
alone, would neither wait for her certificate of birth,
nor her other certificates before they led her wrong.
You see Fanchette's fate! Well, then imagine to
yourself Fanchette becoming a mother, and then
just imagine a little, the fate of the infant she would
bring into the world. No, it is not well done to
have left Fanchette at the mercy of the vagabonds
of the high road, and the wolves of the wilderness.
It is not Christian, it is not human; it may be lawful, I know nothing about that; but I would not
have done it myself, even for fifteen thousand livres
annually and the title of mayor into the bargain!
My poor wife weeps for very shame and scolds me

for not having sought Fanchette before she was taken
to the hospital. Your gossip brandishes her spindle
angrily, and says you must be told all about it. The
Administrator who first gave this pretty piece of advice, held here a very good place under government.
In the very midst of this fine affair, whether the
government knew it or not, he has been withdrawn,
and sent into another town, as Receiver of the
finances, with the advance, so please you, of two
or three thousand livres more to his salary, as the
story goes.

As for us poor people, the moral of the business
for us is, that if we do not succeed in bringing up
our children, if we die in poverty, if we leave them
nfirm or under age to the care of the public chari-
:ies, at the gate of the hospitals behold the help
they will have in this world; behold how the administrators of the public benevolence will watch
over their wants: behold how Christian congrega-
tions will watch over their morals! God of Heaven
and Earth! is it not enough to make one's hair stand
on end?

And now, my dear godfather, I pray God to have
you and all your house in his holy keeping, and that
He may receive you into Heaven, by a path straight
as my goad; whilst for them at the hospital, we
may safely promise *them*, as the saying is that they
shall get there by a road about as straight as my
reaping hook.

BLAISE BONNIN—HUSBANDMAN.

Mayor's Assistant of Montgivret, near la Chatre, (Indre.)

COMMUNICATION.

To the Editor of " La Revue Indépendante."

BEING intrusted by my neighbour Blaise with forwarding this letter to his godfather Claude, and correcting its faults of orthography, I thought, my dear Sir, that the sad and revolting facts of which it contains the ingenuous recital, ought not to remain buried in the correspondence of two illiterate countrymen, who are certainly very ill able to give it the publicity its nature deserves.

Feeling much struck by this almost incredible anecdote, I sought for its proofs, and have acquired the certainty of its being so perfectly true, that I may assert it on my own responsibility. I have reproached my friends, who were almost eye-witnesses of the facts, for not having demanded from public opinion that justice which the tribunals seem to refuse to this crime of lese-charity and lese-humanity. They reply that their deposition had been prepared and sent to the "Siecle" and to two other papers, which had disdained to insert it, also to the "National" who had inserted it, mutilated and weakened, by presenting in the shape of doubts, all that was affirmative. I can conceive the reluctance of a journal to become the guarantee of a fact, so strange, so revolting, and seemingly so improbable, and I know that a Paris life, and the pre-occupation of the daily press, scarcely leave space for the cares of a more minute inquisition. I can also understand the reluctance of my friends in La Chatre to pursue the representatives of opinions opposed to their own with such a terrible accusation; not that the Ægis of conservative doctrines has any terror for them; but in the provinces one is easily suspected of private rancour, or personal prejudice, when the dangerous ground of political difference is entered upon. I stand so completely aloof from all parties; the conservatives and the functionaries of my own province are so entirely unknown to me; in a word, I am such a perfect stranger to all bitterness, to all discussion, to all resentment, that even were I obliged to cite the names of the guilty parties, I should be forced to seek for them, either not knowing them, or having forgotten them. Standing in this position, I have taken upon myself, without scruple, the task of laying open these unheard of details to public opinion; they are attested by a judicial enquiry, set on foot by the Commissary of Police, and given in evidence at the Mansion-house of the city. Three months have passed away without the Attorney-General's thinking fit to prosecute the investigation, and until now the Sub-Prefect has remained indifferent towards deeds, over which he should nevertheless have at least some control.

Of all our magistrates, Monsieur Delavault alone, Mayor and Deputy of La Chatre, has done his duty; but even he has not yet completed it ; for he alone is in a position to demand a reparation to outraged public morality ; and we hope that he will not be contented by the explanations of the members of the hospital board, whose general advice has been to stifle the affair. This honourable magistrate, and these too timorous citizens, will recognize that their true duty lies not in respecting persons, but in respecting public morals, and public faith. The members of the hospital board, selected probably from persons reputed estimable and trustworthy, will have cause to reproach themselves greatly if they accept the responsibility of the abduction of Fanchette. Many of these citizens, perhaps all, are fathers of families. What horror would be theirs if, afflicted by any of those misfortunes which carry disgrace into a family, they should find in the public the same disdain for their complaints, the same contempt for their griefs, the same toleration for the ravishers of their children. Let them not trust too much to their fortune and their consideration in the world, as guaranteeing them from such misfortunes. There are analogous sorrows not less grave ; there are coincidences that one might almost call chastisements from Heaven. Other persons are involved in this adventure. A painful suspicion, perhaps even severe blame, rests with the diligence contractors. But one can hardly believe, that so many accomplices, can so easily, so gratuitously, be united to

commit a crime. The people of the diligence may
have been deceived. They may have been made to
believe that the unfortunate Fanchette had sense
enough to save her from the dangers to which they
abandoned her; they must have had higher authority
to vanquish their repugnance, the expression of
which is avouched in the enquiry. There is in all
this I know not what disgraceful plot, which it belongs to public discussion to unveil, and which the
secondary actors will find it to be their interest,
without doubt, to reveal to justice. As for myself,
I have something of the character of Blaise Bonnin;
like him, I think comparatively little of material
punishments,—I think more of the effect of public
opinion in such matters, and although the part of
moral executioner is hateful to me, although I do
not feel fitted for it in any manner, I would accept
it without hesitation, if I felt it were my mission
to do so.

Certain of finding in your Review as much courage
and impartiality, as I have needed myself to fulfil
my mournful duty, I entrust you with the publica-
tion of this short and too true history, asking pardon
for introducing to your readers a romance so unpoeti-
cal and disagreeable.

· But I must also furnish you with the denouement.
The day before yesterday, a letter from the mayoralty
of Riom (Cantal) gave notice to the mayoralty of
La Chatre of the reappearance of poor Fanchette
upon the scene of social life. She had been recog-
nized by her description, and arrested in the midst

of a troop of wandering jugglers, of which she had
the honour to form a part. They sent her back to
the hospital of La Chatre, *from one station to another,*
that is to say, from prison to prison, alas in what a
state, and in what company! Are there not some
destinies, which almost break the heart?—and has
the skilful and generous author of the Mysteries of
Paris exaggerated the horrors of the misery and
humiliations of the poor and the disinherited. From
what a state of abjectness and pollution was the unhappy Fanchette rescued, to be taken back to the
sisters of the hospital? Is not the venom of prostitution already in the veins of this unhappy creature,
innocent, even in infamy, since she is deprived of
the sense of right or wrong? Will any one say,
that each one must take care of himself, and that
society has no duties to perform towards those who
know not even what duty is? No, no one will say so.
There is not a mother, in that happy station where
honour is so preciously guarded, and modesty so
tenderly protected, who does not feel her heart moved
with grief and indignation at the idea of Fanchette's
miseries. And is there not also something to be
said, even after what has been put forth by the
eighteenth and nineteenth centuries, upon the immorality of celibacy, apropos to the inhuman conduct
of the Lady Superior of the hospital? For such a
counsel to have found acceptance in the bosom of a
woman, vowed, perhaps from vocation, and doubtless from habit, to works of charity, there needs the
secret inspiration of morbid perversity, or the bitter

chagrin of one of those aversions from a woman towards a child, which are sometimes to be met with in old maids.

In the midst of this isolation from all natural, legal and clerical protection, one must take refuge in the hope, too romantic alas! that Fanchette, has found by chance among these BOHEMIANS, the Parias of civilization, that hospitality, that respect and charity which our society and state religion have so strangely withheld from her. Who knows whether God, who so often veils his face to the pharisees, has not extended his paternal care over the straw, where for three months she has slept with the impure family of the *Zingari*. Fatal condition of our society! where a child so abandoned has no succour more immediate than the austere and mysterious protection of heaven. Oh! Providence dost thou deign to work miracles for those struck with imbecility by Thy hand in their very cradle, and whose destiny drags them along the sorrowful wayside of life? Dost thou chace away from the path of the orphan virgin, the infamous procuress who traffics in infancy, and who is seen prowling at night in the cross roads, watching for innocence and weakness in order to force them to corruption, and deliver them up perverted or trembling, to the rich man, to the father of a family, aye, even to the very magistrate of our small cities? small cities! dens of infamy, where intimidation assures impunity to vice and crime, as mystery does at Paris.

Let us turn away our eyes from these spectacles

of iniquity and pray to God for the feeble, since men
are deaf.

GEORGE SAND.

*From the Attorney-General of La Châtre, to the Editor
of " La Revue Indépendante."*

La Chatre, Nov. 9th, 1843.

SIR,

In one of the last numbers of your Journal,
you have inserted an article signed George Sand, in
which the author lays hold of a fact, deplorable,
doubtless, but which is nevertheless very far from
bearing the grave aspect attributed to it, for the
purpose of using it as a subject for unjustifiable
accusations against several functionaries of this
town.

Here, however is the event, so strangely related
by this writer. It is important to show it directly
in its true colours.

During last July, a young girl, almost idiotic, who
had been previously received into the hospital of La
Chatre, and to which she had ceased to belong, suddenly disappeared. The Lady Superior, not in the
intention, as has been stated, of losing the unfortunate child, but on the contrary, in the hope, of restoring her to her family, by sending her to the place
from whence she appeared to have come, had sent
her, by a public conveyance to the environs of
Aubusson, and there she had been deposited and
sheltered in a neighbouring house.

After residing there some days, this young gir fled, and for some time, managed to evade all the re searches of the local authorities.

Such are the facts, in their simplicity, and the re- flections they have suggested to the author of the article are neither just nor well founded.

"The Attorney-General of La Chatre," he says "has remained an indifferent witness." Such an assertion is incorrect on all points.

On the contrary, the most active researches have been instituted by the Chamber of La Chatre, both to find the young girl, and to punish the culpable, if any party be culpable in this affair.

Instructions have been given, an enquiry has taken place, all judicial investigation has been applied, not only as to the conduct of the Lady Superior, but also as to that of the agents who might have given her their aid; and the tribunal, after bestowing its best attention upon the affair, has returned a Judg- ment of *Not Proven*, an evident proof that the facts alleged were not surrounded by the aggravating cir- cumstances with which this writer has been pleased to invest them. Besides, they had been judged of, in the same manner by the Attorney-General for Aubusson, whose attention had been equally directed to the subject.

This is not all: it is to the unceasing efforts of the thamber of La Chatre, that the recovery of the young girl is owing, and it is by my agency that she has been claimed and reinstated provisionally in the hospital of La Chatre, where she still is. She was arrested on the 18th of last August, in the province of Riom, as a mendicant, and placed shortly after, in the hospital of this town.

Such is the exact truth, supported by proofs and evidence, of which I publicly avouch myself the guarantee. Let the author now compare the incredible story, of which his article contains the recital, with this simple statement of facts, and I appeal to his conscience to say, whether he has not made himself the responsible editor of a romance.

I request, and if necessary require you Sir, to be good enough to insert this letter in your next number.

Accept, Sir, the assurance of my
high consideration,
Rochoux,
Attorney-General of La Chalre.

REPLY.

To the Attorney-General of La Châtre.

You are wrong, very much in the wrong, Sir, tc take upon yourself individually a reproach which only weighed upon you collectively, and of which certainly the greatest portion did not fall upon you. Good God, what is it you do? You appeal to my conscience, and you expose the depth of your own, and force me to direct a severe enquiry therein—I, who would gladly have discovered their only faults, if not pardonable, at least reparable, merely forgetfulness, indifference, youthful levity, pre-occupation of mind. But instead of this, must I tell you what I could see now, if I did not endeavour to excuse you, and if it did not wound me deeply to condemn a young magistrate and my countryman?

But is it then decreed by Heaven, that in the present time, all indulgence to the culpable is impossible? You have descended into an arena, where I cannot see you make your first essay in arms, without the deepest grief for the weakness of your cause. You provoke new explanations before the public, you challenge me to single combat by a contradiction, which I cannot submit to, not that it touches me, not that it wounds me, but because when once on the pursuit of truth, no retreat is possible. On the part of the authorities of La Chatre, there have been menaces of proceedings against the author of *Fanchette*. The author of *Fanchette*, has nothing to fear from a tribunal which would be at once party and judge. He feels sure that these menaces are nothing but friendly efforts at intimidation, which they would blush at carrying into execution, and that if they were executed they would provoke investigations which would give too much force and notoriety to the truth of his assertions, to the scrupulous reality of the *romance* of Fanchette. Therefore, sir, I will not look upon your letter to "La Revue Independante," as a snare laid for my good faith; an attorney-general surely stands in too high a position to descend to that of a mere agent or spy. I will therefore accept this discussion, and answer you, as you challenge me, in all simplicity.

You commence by avowing that the fact I have *laid hold* of is *deplorable* doubtless. No, I have not laid hold of the fact, it is the fact which has laid hold of me, and overwhelmed my mind and heart; in the same way that the same fact lays hold of you, and forces you at once to qualify it as *deplorable*. I have no need here to make an appeal to your conscience. I can see that it is touched and harassed, and the very first stroke of your pen protests naively against all that is to follow. I am not doubting your sincerity in this—I have pleasure in doing justice to you.

But you assert that I have *stated strangely* an event

which you take upon yourself *to restore to its true character*. Well then, I must resume my narrative, and compare it with yours, and you will see that your apology for the guilty parties is in itself the confirmation of my accusations. You find no *aggravating circumstances* in this *(deplorable)* adventure—but I see a crime; a crime for which a new name must be invented, *innocenticide*.

I said, that a young idiotic girl . . . . . you say *almost idiotic;* I repeat, idiotic to the point of not knowing how to speak even, although she is neither deaf nor dumb; idiotic to the point of not being either able to tell who she is, whence she comes, nor even what she wants. It is no semi-idiocy to be deprived of the notion of one's own existence, and the appreciation of one's own individuality.

But let us pass that. Had I wished to write a romance, as you reproach me, unintentionally I suppose, with intending to do, (you know well that romance writing is my trade, and that no one need blush for his trade,) I should have represented Fanchette as less of an idiot than she really is. That would have made her more interesting to my readers. Fanchette herself would indeed be an interesting heroine of romance, with her vacant mouth and haggard eyes! It would have been a very poor invention.

The utterly idiotic Fanchette then, found in the meadow Burat, as I have already stated, taken into the hospital in compliance with a written order from Doctor Boursault, and afterwards placed with a person named Thomas, by a woman called Landat, whose trade it is to house lost and abandoned children.—Fanchette returning to the hospital, from the fact of her very idiocy preventing her from appreciating the disgust she caused there, disappeared one fine morning without the doctor, Monsieur Boursault's ticket of exit, a formality *required*, but which they very well knew how to do without.

This is my version; you, less prolix than myself, for you have the honour not to be a *writer* by profession, say simply that Fanchette, *having ceased to belong to the hospital, and having returned* there, SUDDENLY DISAPPEARED. Suddenly disappeared, that is not going away naturally, that is not being regularly transferred into a new asylum, that is not leaving according to regulations, with the exit ticket from the doctor. the sanction of the administrators, the order of the prefect; in fact, to disappear suddenly, is to flee, to commit suicide, to be abducted, or assassinated. If the attorney-general, the sub-prefect or the priest had just disappeared suddenly, there would have been much more excitement in the town, and with good reason. But no one ought to disappear suddenly, without the local authorities enquiring, suddenly also, as to the whereabouts of the vanished individual.

In fact, none amongst us, however much of an idiot, has the right to disappear suddenly; and the attorney-general knows that well.

The Commissary of Police says, and I say with him, that Fanchette *disappeared* during the first days of July, and the Report, dated the 31st July, states three times, as the date of the event, *about a month since;* you say it happened *during the month,* we agree pretty well as to dates. The tribunal gave in its judgment of *not proven* the 15th September. Fanchette was found on the 18th August; she had then been lost only for about six weeks—not enough apparently to expose either her morals or her life to any danger. The tribunal only sought for and obsolved the delinquents, after the lapse of two months and a half; it has not been indiscreetly precipitate. We agree pretty well, I repeat, Mr. Attorney-General.

I take up my report, drawn from the *romance* of the Commissary of Police, from the extremely *romantic* deposition of Thomas Desroys, the conductor of the diligence (Blaise Bonnin wrote patache from an old habit) and the replies of two women, the postmistresses, and who have undertaken also in our district, the contract for the diligences—" *One of these ladies was sent for to the hospital by the Lady Superior; and having gone there, the Lady Superior said to her, that some persons, strangers without doubt, had abandoned a young girl in this town, aged about fourteen or fifteen,* DEPRIVED ENTIRELY OF ALL INTELLIGENCE; *that they had cast her upon the hospital, and that she intended to use similar means to disembarrass herself of the child; that consequently the girl was to be placed in the coach going to Aubusson, with an order to the conductor* TO GET RID OF HER *before her arrival at Aubusson, and to* LEAVE HER ON THE ROAD; *and* *that no one might be aware of it, she would send her out of the town by the servant: this commission was undertaken by Madame****. These two ladies add, that it was with extreme repugnance they undertook such an affair, but that in virtue of the character of the Lady Superior, they yielded to her* REITERATED REQUEST."*

* Copy of the enquiry made by order of the Mayor of La Chatre, by the Commissary of Police in this town.

31st July, 1843.

The undersigned, Commissary of Police for the town of La Chatre, (Indre), by virtue of a letter from the mayor, dated yesterday, which ordered new investigations as to the facts which preceded, accompanied, or followed the exposure of a young girl, a stranger and idiotic who had been received into our care about a month since, and who was afterwards placed in the hospital of the town ; obedient to this order and having learned that this child had disappeared through the medium of the diligence of Monsieur Chauvet, post master, we went to his office, and found there Mesdames Chauvet, and Gazonneau, who, in answer to our questions, declared and affirmed, that about a month before, Madame Gazonneau, had been sent for to the Hospital of the town by the Lady Superior ; that having gone there, the Lady Superior had told her that some persons, strangers without doubt, had abandoned a young girl about fourteen or fifteen, who was wholly without intellect, that they had cast her upon the hospital, and that to disembarrass herself of the child, she should use similar means ; that, consequently, she must be placed in the diligence going to Aubusson, with an order to the conductor *to get rid of her before his arrival at Aubusson, by curing her on the high road,* and that no one might know of it, she would send her by a servant out of the town, upon the high road : which commission was undertaken by Madame Gazonneau. The two ladies add, that it was with extreme repugnance they

It is impossible to be more explicit.   Now let
Thomas Desroys and the *romantic* pen of the Com-
missary of Police, speak for themselves.   He (Thomas
Desroys) declared to us, that about a month since,
Madame **** said to him, "just outside the town,
you will see upon the high road, a little girl who is
an IDIOT conducted by a servant of the hospital.
SHE WILL NOT BE INSCRIBED UPON THE LIST OF TRA-
VELLERS.   SHE IS A CHILD WHOM THEY WISH TO HAVE
LOST.   Therefore when you are about a league from
Aubusson you will make her get down from the
diligence. and ABANDON her on the high road," and
that in fact, when he arrived near a place called
Chaussidout, about a league from Aubusson, he
made her get down from the diligence, ABANDONED
her, and obeyed PUNCTUALLY the orders which had
been given to him.

undertook such an affair, but that in virtue of her character as
Lady Superior they yielded to her reiterated request.

We have also questioned the said Thomas Desroys, the conductor attached to the administration of M Chauvet, Postmaster.
He has declared to us, that just when he was starting for
Aubusson, about a month since, Madame Gazonneau said to
him, "You will find upon the high road, a short way out of the
town, a little girl, an idiot, conducted by a servant of the hospital of La Chatre; she will not be inscribed on the list, she is a
child whom they wish to lose.   Therefore, when you are about
a mile from Aubusson, you will make her get down from the
diligence, and leave her on the road"—that in fact, when arrived
at a village called Chaussidout, about a mile from Aubusson, he
made her get down, left her, and obeyed the orders which had
been given to him exactly.

La Chatre, same date.
(Signed,)   BOUVER, Commissary of Police.

Thus ends the first enquiry. Every one knows that the first depositions are the most trustworthy. There has been no time for consultation, for influence to be used, for the consequences of the deed to be understood and dreaded. And why should Thomas Desroys have drawn back? He has himself perhaps no very large development of his intellectual powers. He obeyed, conscientiously, *punctually*, the orders of his superiors. And why should the postmistresses have hesitated to throw the blame where it ought to fall? They felt *extremely repugnant* to obey, and *the character of the superior* alone reassured them.

Now, let it be remarked that it is no longer Blaise Bonnin, no longer George Sand, but the Commissary of Police, whose official *romance* agrees so perfectly with the one which the attorney-general deigns to offer us. This last romance, more concise, and more rapid, is certainly the best composed of the two. That of the Commissary of Police is rude and simple as the fact; that of the attorney-general is woven much more artfully. It glides over the facts, and developes the motives. It enters into the secret thoughts of people, and acquits them on the ground of their intentions, as formerly men were prosecuted for their intentions.

"*The Lady Superior,*" he says, "*not with the intention of losing this unfortunate being, as has been said* (as the deponents have said to the Commissary of Police, as the Superior herself said to the deponents, as the Commissary of Police has declared in the re-

port, as every body knows, and as Blaise Bonnin
and George Sand have repeated) *but on the contrary
in the* HOPE, *by sending her back to the place she appeared to have come from, of finding out her family,
has caused her to be transferred by a public conveyance to the environs of Aubusson, and there, she
had been deposited, and sheltered in a neighbouring
house.''*

I like this version, it has certainly more grace and
delicacy than the brutal responses of Thomas Desroys.
But the fact remains the same, the manner of telling
it alters nothing. The narration of the attorney-
general is doubtless the result of an enquiry set on
foot by him six weeks after that of the Commissary
of Police, and the replies of the Lady Superior (even
if she had ever been interrogated.)

Thus the Superior has fully justified herself, by
declaring that she had the *hope* of restoring Fanchette
to her family. But this supposition of a family for
Fanchette was rather gratuitous, since Fanchette
disappeared from Chaussidout as she had disappeared
from La Chatre, carried off, perhaps by gipsies, perhaps by other nuns, but of course always with the
hope of causing her to recover her family. If the
report of the tribunal has proved that Fanchette was
deposited at and received in a neighbouring house, if
there was a house near the scene of the crime—it
must have been a pang of conscience, a good impulse
of Thomas Desroys', and I thank him for it from my
heart—such a thing has often been seen in many a
fable, and many a romance. Œdipus, Romulus,

Cyrus, Genevieve, de Brabant, many a hero of anti-
quity, many a heroine of a fairy tale, has been confided to the care of a squire, of a soldier, of a ruffian
charged to drown, to strangle or to hang them, and
almost always, these honest scoundrels, these sensi-
tive murderers, either touched by compassion or
seized by remorse, have left to chance the victim
condemned to perish, or given to shepherds, the child
they were enjoined to leave to the mercy of the
waves, of robbers, or of wild beasts. It has even
been seen, in poetical history, that wolves and does
have united in the good work, and suckled the abandoned children, which only proves that brutes are
less cruel than men, or to speak as Blaise Bonnin
would speak, that valets are not so *worse* as their
masters.

And I should have been glad, both for the honour
of a man of the people, and for the satisfaction of
our hearts, Mr. Attorney-General, that Thomas
Desroys *had* disobeyed his orders, that he had sought
a house, that he had found one in the above-named
place, (of course you have been to the spot since,
to see whether by chance, it was not a forest, or a
desert place?) in fact, that Fanchette had been received into some house, but the first depositions of
Thomas Desroys neither make mention of this house,
nor of its hospitable inhabitants.

It must either be that the said Thomas was very
much afraid of being rebuked for his disobedience,
or that his Christian humility reaches the point of
not even letting his good actions be suspected. Perhaps you have succeeded in drawing this avowa-

from him; you have done well. You believed it,
you recognize him for a sincere and God-fearing
man; therefore he did not lie, when in the former
enquiry, he declared he had been ordered to *abandon
a child, and let it be lost?* And doubtless he has not
retracted this point, in the second enquiry which
you have instituted, and the result of which we
do not know as yet, but which you promise that we
shall see.

Well then, Mr. Attorney-General, this is what
we demand of you, this, and nothing less; an explanation or justification of the impunity guaranteed
until now by the tribunal to a fact which appeared
to us so atrocious. Do you think that we shall rejoice and triumph if unfortunately the report of the
Commissary of Police is entirely true, if the wit-
nesses spoke the truth in their first depositions, if
the public outcry is well founded, if the Mayor has
acted wisely in prosecuting this enquiry, if our indignation is just, and our complaints reasonable?
Alas! no, we shall be sad enough, you, I, the magistrates, the functionaries, the guilty parties, the wit-
nesses and the public. Every one will be horror-
stricken, humiliated at seeing humanity so perverse,
religion so debased, weakness so neglected, misery
so despised; none of us will raise a cry of victory,
believe me. But you know this well, you know
that we are not hypocrites, you know that we do
not delight in useless scandal; you know well that
the writer who is now addressing you, has never
declaimed against individuals, and takes no active
part in politics. Why do you declaim thus, apropos

of a fact so utterly estranged from all politics? Why
try to extenuate the horror of such a crime, you,
whose mission should be to pursue and punish crime,
whilst ours, should rather be to weep sometimes
over the rigour of the law and the fate of the guilty?
The part, which you assume to-day, is not comprised,
in the duties of your position. No superior power
can have dictated it to you, and if such a power did
exist, you would be the first to struggle against it.
Hesitate no longer therefore to appease the sorrowful indignation which has seized upon your fellow
citizens, and to explain to them satisfactorily the
indulgence of the tribunal; they will accept this
gratefully, they will rejoice to find that no one is
really to blame; and I myself will be the first to
say to my readers, "Yes, it was a romance, I was
deceived. Do not imagine Fanchette a true story,
thanks be to God, it is not. It was a miserable
dream, and nothing more."

But if such be your intention Mr. Attorney-
General, it is not realized. The explanations you
have been kind enough to offer us, are not satisfactory; on the contrary, we see in them the avowal,
the confirmation of the sad events which have already made us suffer so much. A Lady Superior,
arguing, according to you, that *the child has ceased
to belong to the hospital*, seizes upon her, causes her
to be abducted .... *transferred* if you like, but with
great secrecy, the fact is proved, and you do not
deny it; *transferred* whither? *to the place whence she
appeared to have come*. But you do not know whence,
the child has never told it. She could not tell it,

M

she could not speak : no one knew her, no one knows
her now, you have never been able to discover who
she is. The Lady Superior has said, that *from her
costume, she supposed she was a Marchoise.* On this
well defined certainty, she has been *transferred* upon
the high road to some wild place near *the environs of
Aubusson,* not in any designated house. Your version relates, " *And there* (on the high road, in some
place or other) *she had been set down, and received
in a neighbouring house.*" Now is all this regular,
evident, conceivable, or logical? No, all this is
neither conceivable, nor evident, nor satisfactory,
nor sincere. It is the awkward apology of a guilty
conscience. I can never comprehend, and no one
else can be made to comprehend, how the tribunal
could have been satisfied with it, or that you should
content yourself with it, and no one will say with
you that the verdict of " not proven" is a manifest
proof of the innocence of the accused.

No, *all the investigations of justice have not been
brought to bear, both upon the conduct of the Lady
Superior, and upon that of the agents who might have
lent her their aid.* No, a hundred times no, for these
agents would not be worthy of faith, if their second
depositions has destroyed the first, and this first deposition is overwhelming, it admits of no reply. No
jury would find there any extenuating circumstances.
The Attorney-General of Aubusson, whose authority
you invoke,—

　　　　One wonders how in *such* affair
　　　　Such a name should e'er get there—

can have nothing to tell us as to a fact which is not

within his jurisdiction, and which does not neces-
sarily come under his cognizance. No one has been
pleased to clothe the fact with aggravating circumstances,
such an office could give pleasure to no one. The
whole affair has made me ill with grief. I am not
accustomed, as your fraternity of magistrates are, to
weigh in the hollow of a cold hand, the iniquities of
my fellow men.

I have invented nothing, but who knows that
better than yourself? You make an appeal to my
conscience, and I call upon yours thrice over! Conscience! conscience! conscience! slumbering conscience of Mr. Attorney-General, awake, and be
again what God first formed you!

But let us support our case by your own testimony;
it is from your own words we wish to deduce the
proof of the crime the wickedness, which the law
qualifies by the name of *exposition.* You say at first,
" Fanchette has been *transferred to the environs of
Aubusson, and there, deposited and received into a neighbouring house.—Neighbouring* to what?—To the
environs of Aubusson? Surely that is rather vague
—and besides *deposited* and *sheltered* are two expres-
sions, rather contradictory; a deposit is *received*, as
of right, but anything which is abandoned or
neglected, is *sheltered.* More than this, had it been
a deposit, a regular thing, and not a clandestine exposure, the conductor of a public vehicle would not
have been charged with it—but one of those persons,
who like the woman Lanast, are employed by
authority in such matters; and at least if a man
not in any public function had been employed, he

would have had a sum of money given to him, for the maintenance of the child, and not the reward, for his blind simplicity only; he would have had one of those houses pointed out to him, which are specially intended as places of refuge for lost children, and if need is, for their brethren in misfortune, idiots; and not the first house he might happen to see, *near the environs of Aubusson.* Besides, in no such case could the authorisation of the Prefect have been dispensed with, for even if the supposed family of Fanchette had gone to the hospital to claim her, she would not have been given up to her parents without this formality. Thus then, Mr. Attorney-General, you are entangled by your own avowal, and if you permit me to quote Latin, even I who do not know it, to you who are certainly well acquainted with it, I shall say to you, *Habemus confitentem reum.*

Another overwhelming proof against the sincerity and good faith of your pretended *deposit,* is, that Fanchette has been so far from being *sheltered,* that in reply to the inquiries set on foot by the authorities of La Chatre, the mayor of St. Maixent, under whose jurisdiction Chaussidout is, has declared in an official letter, that *notwithstanding the most anxious researches,* he had been able to discover nothing as to this young girl. She had neither been seen, nor heard of at Chassidout, in the *Commune of St. Maixent, notwithstanding the anxious researches of the mayor!!!* Then she cannot have been sheltered any where, but must have been abandoned on the high road, whatever may be said to the contrary. If we were taking up this matter either in the spirit of romance or calumny (it appears that it is one and the same) we should ask Mr. Attorney-General to conduct us to this invisible and unfindable house, which is chosen by the hospital of La Chatre to accommodate its surplus patients, and we would also summon Mr. Attorney-General to receive the attestations of the inhabitants of this fantastic dwelling, in whose care, according to him, Fanchette was *deposited*.

We have not finished yet. *After having resided several days in this imaginary house,* where, even if we accept Mr. Attorney-General's affirmative, Fanchette would have had no right to claim an asylum, since another had been designed for her by the prefect; in *this household* which was not in the least accustomed to the care of a lost child, a charge which would have been a burden impossible for them to accept, and which certainly no one there would have had the time, nor means, nor even the obligation to keep and watch over; in this house, you say, *this young girl succeeded in withdrawing herself from all the researches of the local authorities.* This is false; you have been deceived. Fanchette, who has never been capable of putting two words together rationally, is certainly not a person who could *succeed in withdrawing* herself from any thing whatever. Much she is likely to know about the local authorities! She is very likely to withdraw herself, poor thing, she who seeks an asylum against cold and hunger like a dog that has lost its master. It is very easy to understand what the poor wanderer wanted when she quitted her new lodging, she desired to go back

to the hospital. That was her one idea. We cannot
even imagine that she had any other, since she did
nothing else when with the woman Thomas. Unhappy indeed was she, to fancy she should there find
succour and protection. Oh! what poniards her
blind confidence ought to thrust into the Lady Superior's heart, if this woman has a heart! But the
shame of reprobation and the fear of punishment,
awake a sort of conscience, such as it is, amongst
those who otherwise would have none. May she
weep and pray at the feet of Christ, this so called
Sister of Charity; this is my prayer for her. I wish
her no further punishment.

Thus, it must be evident, that Fanchette could
not, like a bandit, or escaped galley slave, *withdraw
herself from the researches of authority.* She was
ignorant of all authority, she knew nothing but the
high road; she may have followed it by chance,
hoping to get back to La Chatre. She met some
gipsies, they carried her off, with her good will or
against it, who knows? She was found six weeks
after that, amongst a troop of itinerant jugglers, at
Riom. You say, she had given herself up to men-
dicancy; it is possible, but with whom? You do
not tell us, and yet you ought to know. *You do
know.* All this has appeared to some people here, a
romantic invention, an ingenious pretence. Yet it is
nothing but simply natural. There are none but
jugglers in France to whom a child could be useful;
they are the persons who pick up, or shelter those
whom the hospital rejects.

By your *care,* by your *agency she has been provi-*

sexually reinstated at the Hospital of La Chatre. I do not doubt it: but let us know also, by whose order, by whose care was it, that this unhappy child was brought back, as a malefactor, and amongst malefactors, sleeping with them probably on their straw, or the pavement of a prison?

We all know what such a journey must be? in such company, and if instead of merely idiotic, Fanchette has become mad, and if she is pregnant, as they say, (but which L do not myself believe,) if she is already infected with the horrors of debauchery and prostitution, at whose door must the fault be laid? *And no one is guilty?* and your *verdict of not proven* as to this *deplorable* fact is a *manifest proof of it!* And is it to us you say this? to us, mothers of families? Have you a sister, a mother, a wife? And I am a romancer? Ah! what are you but a romancer? If it is a disgrace, you must drink from the same cup.

I pray your pardon! my heart bleeds at being forced to speak thus to you; but what had you to do in this affair? Was my accusation against your carelessness as a magistrate as heavy as this with which you have charged yourself so foolishly, so uselessly?

The facts which you adduce, confirm mine. The only difference, I repeat, is in the manner in which you appreciate them, since you do not recognize in their features *the gravity which we attribute to them.* I never said that you had a heart of stone, I did not think it. I should never have dared to tax you with insensibility, with contempt for human nature, with partiality towards criminals, with aversion towards those who detest crime. And yet, to hear you, to read your letter, one would believe that you had this moral ice in your soul, and all this perversity in your intellect. You have been too confident; you know that we recognize you as a good-hearted though a weak young man, and your zeal to justify this *deplorable* event has made you forget that the public to which you address yourself, the unpolished—almost uncivilized—public, who judges a man by his words, and troubles itself neither about his secret instincts nor private life, would condemn you without appeal, and would meet your apology with an anathema. We shall even be forced to defend you, and we will do it, whilst you accuse us of provoking a scandal, and of blackening your intentions.

You fancy yourself compromised by our reproaches of slowness and patience. Well, then, you should have contented yourself with this justification : "we *have* acted, we *did* endeavour to find Fanchette." You should have said, that you, personally, set the enquiry on foot, and that the rest was not your affair, since the verdict of " not proven" did not emanate from you; and you should not have made yourself the *responsible editor* of such an improbable *romance* as that entitled the *Hope* of the Lady Superior. This is indeed the *incredible* part of the story ! The solicitude of this woman who takes the child away from the surveillance of the authorities, from the care of the doctor, from an asylum chosen by the prefect, from a secure refuge, from the succour accorded by the government, and all this through goodness of heart, and who causes the child to be lost *at a part of the country* where she *presumes*, where she *hopes* that she *ought* to have a family, and where *she might be able* to find it again. How ingenious is all this! what enlightened charity! what candour of intention!

Thanks to God! I am a woman, and understand nothing of the laws which men have invented, but I have heard that there are punishments for those who cause death by imprudence. Is there not also a punishment for those who risk the health, the life, the honour of others by imprudence? Let us agree that in this case there has been nothing worse; even then the imprudence is grave enough, and if the Lady Superior is not punished, which God forbid,— I am no advocate for the system of punishments—at least she merits some severe reprimand; at least, she cannot deserve that a magistrate should take her part, and declare her innocent and persecuted, well intentioned and free from all reproach; at least we have the right to be astonished, to blame, and to demonstrate one to the other the horror and scandal of an imprudence of this kind. What! you conceal, you stifle the affair? certainly! use your freedom! but you are enraged when we discover it, and you wish to forbid us even its discussion. Are we in France or Russia?

You are angry with me for having said that you, Mr. Attorney-General, had remained *a passive witness*. Well, if you have not been passive, so much the better. I believe you from my soul. But why then take up the position of an impassioned apologist of the most culpable intention ? That is even worse.

You have used every effort to recover Fanchette . I believe it entirely. The other functionaries have also acted with activity, with a great fear of the scandal which was threatening to fall upon the administration of the hospital, and upon the clergy : I believe this also ! But the lost one found, such as she is, in whatever state, you are all suddenly calm again ! The Under-Prefect has been much affected, I am told, by Fanchette's fate ; I do not doubt the goodness of his heart. But are the most honourable and best of men obliged, *by reason of their trade*, to this mysterious sort of prudence, as soon as they are invested with public duties? Is it the spirit of the góvernment which imposes upon them this indulgence for certain persons, and this irritation against others ? They tell me so; but I will not believe it. Meanwhile a modest subscription was opened at La Chatre for the purpose of printing and selling for the benefit of Fanchette, the *romance* which bears her name. This was a good work. The pretended romance had met with success in the locality. The printer ran no risk in the reproduction of a work already printed, and not prohibited by the government. The price was agreed upon, the number of copies fixed. But after having been to the Under-Prefect's Office to enter his declaration (of the printing of the book) he returned quite frightened, and quite decided not to give us the aid of his industry. Mr. Attorney-General, ask the Under-Prefect from me why he has thus intimidated the

honest printer? What did the greater or less publicity of the *romance* of Fanchette matter to him?
If he had exclaimed against the trifling wrong I
might have done him, I should have had great pleasure in unsaying my words and repairing my injustice. But how can we believe in his sincerity,
how can I judge of his intentions, now that I see
him armed with the thunders of intimidation, and
they even say with a menace of prosecution against
myself? At least they ought to allow me the time
to look around and sell my *romance* for the idiot's
benefit, since they allowed to those who lost her,
nine or ten weeks of respite, before any proceedings
were instituted against their conduct.* You will
see that *they* have not been proceeded against with
so much haste and distrust. This is another little
recital of which I again make myself the *responsible
Editor*.

M. Delaveau, Mayor of La Chatre, and Deputy of
L'Indre, on his return from the last session, found in
the court of the Mayoralty, a letter from the Under-
Prefect, which had come in his absence a month or
six weeks before, which letter related to the fact of
Fanchette's disappearance, and demanded an explanation of it. As President of the Board of Admi-

* The attempt was also made to print Fanchette at Bourges,
and failed there from the same causes. Of three printers, one
had the monopoly of the printing for the prefecture, the other
that of the judicial announcements, and the third is printer to
the clergy. At Chateauroux, there was a certainty of the same
obstacles : every where in the provinces, we find the printers in
the same position, in the same dependance on power—and the
same eagerness in power *to paralyze the press*.

nistration of the Hospital, M. Delaveau assembled
the council, and exhorted his colleagues to pay some
attention to the letter of the Under-Prefect. He
received for answer, that they had not replied to the
letter. for as the said letter had not been followed up
by a letter of *reminder*, that is to say a proof of the
determination of this functionary to know the rights
of the case, there was no necessity to think any more
about it. Apparently, said they, the Under-Prefect
is now easy about Fanchette's fate. Monsieur Delaveau was astonished and indignant at his inaction.
He ought not to have been astonished. A member
of this council, zealous for the government, and influential in the affairs of the hospital, had himself
given to the Lady Superior the advice, they even
say the *order*, to have the child lost, and the greater
number of the other members do not appear to have
been much revolted at this deed, since they join
with him in stifling its publicity. But M. Delaveau
did not allow himself to be convinced by the opinion
of the council, nor was he discouraged by the cyni-
cal indifference of certain other persons.

He declared, that since they paralysed his power
of action as President of the Board of Administration of the Hospital, he must confine himself to
acting as mayor, and as such to direct a pursuit
against the guilty parties. It was then that M. Delaveau instituted the enquiry through the Commissary of Police, which I have already cited. It is
short and incomplete, since the Superior and her
adviser do not make their appearance in person.
Nevertheless it suffices to establish the fact clearly,

and a copy of it was sent by the Mayor of La Chatre to the Attorney-General and Under-Prefect. On the same day, the 31st July, the letter of reminder came from the Under-Prefect.

From all this it results that the first movement in the affair, in the absence of M. Delaveau, came from the Under-Prefect, and that after the proceedings set on foot by M. Delaveau, the steps taken by the Under-Prefect had not long to be waited for. Nevertheless, one may doubt whether the letter of reminder would have been sent, if the enquiry had not already taken place. In these circumstances, there is neither a halter nor a crown deserved by the Under-Prefect, but all the merit of activity, courage, and perseverance, is due to M. Delaveau as Mayor, and to M. Boursault as doctor to the hospital : as to the verdict of the tribunal; the most tardy of all, *that* came in just in time to reduce all to nothingness again. You say, Mr. Attorney-General, that this verdict is a *manifest proof* of the *nothingness* of the affair ; but in *our* opinion. it is as yet a manifest proof of the interest that was felt to have it hushed up, *and nothing more.* It is possible that we deceive ourselves ; enlighten us, deign to furnish us with proofs, we desire nothing better than to be convinced by them, if they are good. For myself, I repeat, I am ready to ask pardon for my irreverence, and to retract it publicly, but your letter forces me to persevere in my accusations yet more strongly, because your enormity is itself weighed down by a complete moral nullity. and in no way weakens the gravity of that of the Commissary of Police. And if you wish me

to tell you the reason, it is that the persons who
could have thrown the most light upon your relation
do not figure in it. Thus, you have neither heard
M. Delaveau, mayor of the town, nor his colleagues,
who presided over the council in his absence, nor
M. Boursault, doctor to the hospital, who by his
functions was charged with the duty of giving the
exit ticket, the indispensable authority for the dis-
mission of Fanchette from the hospital. Had the
mayor of La Chatre been summoned, he could have
produced the letter from the mayor of Saint Maixent,
which destroys, without any hope, your illusion as
to the famous house of refuge, *near the environs of
Aubusson*, upon which all the justification of this
deplorable event hangs. Had M Boursault been
interrogated, he could also have destroyed your
charitable illusion as to the *almost idiocy* of the
victim. Besides you ought to have summoned the
woman Cruchon, who lives on the route to Gueret,
and in whose house, Pelagie the servant of the hospital stationed herself with Fanchette whilst waiting
for Thomas Desroys at the moment of the abduction.
As for Desroys himself, we cannot know what he
may have said to you in your interrogation with
closed doors, which may have destroyed the effect of
his first revelations, but we do know what he said
even *yesterday*, which bears all the character of the
simple truth. He had *abandoned* the child on the
high road, in the middle of the night, and his *heart
had become quite heavy* all in a minute without well
knowing why. He had galloped his horses down
the descent, both to flee from Fanchette, and his

own remorse, but suddenly he arrested their progress, as if himself arrested by God's hand, to look whether by running after him, she *might not have come to some harm.* He did not see her, and not being able to get her idea out of his memory, for five or six days he kept asking on his daily journey, of all the country people he met, "*Have you not found a child about here?*"

I have only one error in Blaise Bonnin's letter to rectify; it is that the town of Riom is not in the department of Cantal, it appears that it is in the Puy de Dome. This is a geographical fault which I did not perceive in transcribing the letter: and for this reason, that I know no more about geography than he does. But peasants and women, learned enough perhaps in matters of feeling, are thought fit for nothing better.

Accept, Mr. Attorney-General, the expression of my distinguished respects, &c.

Nohant, near La Chatre.

GEORGE SAND.

Copy of the Letter addressed to George Sand by M. Delaveau, Mayor of La Châtre, and Deputy of l'Indre.

La Chatre, 16th Nov. 1843.

MADAME,

I have just received the communication of your reply to the Attorney-General, attached to the tribune of this town, and the request you make for

my attestation as to the exactitude of the facts in
your history of Fanchette.

As a magistrate, I owed an account of these facts
as much to the Under-Prefect, as to the Attorney-
General of the province, and this duty fulfilled, I
should have been glad to remain a stranger to these
debates, but since you invoke my testimony, I think
it a duty not to withhold homage from the truth.
Therefore I declare that the facts you state in your
reply to the Attorney-General are, in all that relates
to me, of an entire exactitude. As to the extracts
from the enquiry carried on through my requisition,
by the Commissary of Police, they are identical with
the report itself.

Be pleased to accept Madame the assurance of my
highest respect.

(Signed)   DELAVEAU.

*Copy of the Letter addressed to George Sand by M.
Boursault, Doctor to the Hospital of La Châtre.*

MADAME,

You have sent me your reply to the Attorney
General of La Chatre; after having read it, I certif
that in all that relates to me it is of the most perfec
exactitude.

I beg you to accept my respectful salutation.

(Signed)   BOURSAULT, D.M.P

www.ingramcontent.com/pod-product-compliance
Lightning Source LLC
Chambersburg PA
CBHW030557040726
47497CB00008B/2766